The Inn

The Black

Volume 3

This is a work of fiction. Similarities to real people, places, or events are entirely coincidental.

THE INNER CIRCLE

First edition. October 31, 2024.

ISBN: 979-8227801425

Written by Valerius Laborem.

Table of Contents

To my mother, the person whom I treasure most in my heart.

In the age of gods and mortals, there stood a colossal tower piercing the heavens. This magnificent structure was the creation of Abell, the supreme deity, a being of immense power and wisdom. When Abell presented his creation, he vowed to grant a single wish to any mortal who could reach its summit. The challenge was laid, and the call to ascend the Tower echoed throughout the land.

—The Tower of Abell

The Characters And Story Thus Far

After narrowly escaping the clutches of the Sellsword knights in Amacedia, the Black Raven Guild began their journey towards the secret dungeon that would take them to the first floor boss room. However, their journey was cut short when a Bounty Hunter sent by Glimmer's father, named Vanhiel, captured Glimmer and teleported to the city of Denzen, the House of Wind.

Renald and Whisperclaw snuck into Denzen in an attempt to find and save Glimmer. Meanwhile Ironvine, Goldenclaw, and Liaz traveled with King, the wild King Boar, in order to secure an escape route for the others in Denzen. Glimmer met with his father again for the first time since he ran away from home to find his brother Glam.

Upon arriving in the city, Renald, Whisperclaw, and Glimmer found themselves in the midst of a coup against Glimmer's father by the members of the Inner Circle. After trying to fight their way out of the city, all three of them ended up getting captured by the members of the Inner Circle. Liaz, Goldenclaw, and Ironvine fight a pair of statues, one of which is of the Goddess Celestria. Upon defeating them, the trio discovered a chest full of teleportation feathers.

Now Renald, Whisperclaw, and Glimmer are facing a royal execution and the balance of all Bounty Hunter society is on the brink of total collapse. The story moves forward into the

1

next act and our heroes may have to face an even more treacherous journey ahead.

Renald - Renald Black is a 5 ft 8, fit, olive skinned, half-human half-senat man with shaggy black hair swept back like a lion's mane, the signature golden eyes of the esteemed House Black, and two black ram horns growing out of his head. He has a pair of infernal wings, dark vision, and explorer's instincts. He is Self-Centered Chaotic and is a master of using his sword and shield. Renald is also exceptionally skilled in combat, whether with weapons or hand-to-hand. He knows how to strike precisely and exploit weaknesses. He is insatiably inquisitive, always eager to explore new places, uncover hidden secrets, and learn more about the world. He values courage and bravery, and is always ready to face danger head-on to protect his friends and accomplish noble quests.

Ironvine - Ironvine is a 6 ft 5 Chim-Chi with the build of a gorilla with purple fur. Always seeking new thrills and challenges, he has an insatiable wanderlust and a love for the unknown. He values self-sufficiency and freedom, often resisting authority or any form of control that may limit his personal choices. Ironvine is a pacifist and knows pharmaceutical alchemy.

Whisperclaw - Whisperclaw is a 5 ft 3, slim Jackal with sandy brown, spotted fur. She is actually from the far away country of Keyona, which is located on the western continent of Arbedos. Her time in the city prison caused her to become addicted to smoking Luminara Dreamleaf, which she keeps a pouch of at all times. She can constantly be seen with a Dreamleaf roll in her mouth or behind her ear, waiting to be lit. Whisperclaw excels in moving silently and remaining unseen.

THE INNER CIRCLE

Glimmer - Glimmer is a 3 ft tall snargle. He has blue skin and pointy ears, boasting emerald green eyes and razor sharp teeth. His magnetic personality rallies others to his cause, guided by a strict code of honor that values integrity, truthfulness, and unwavering promises. Resistant to change and new ideas, he prefers to adhere to familiar methods, even in the face of evolving circumstances or advice from others. He is Self-Centered, has a knack for playing tricks and pranks, is very nimble, and can see in the dark.

Goldenclaw - Goldenclaw is a one eyed, golden furred saber who was once the ranger for the wilderness between Amacedia and the tower's exit. That was until he helped the Black Raven Guild steal back Vesper's Ethereal Enchantment Scroll from Blackthorn. Now he is acting as the group's companion and guide while they travel towards the Secret Dungeon that will take them to the Floor 1 Boss Room.

Liaz - Liaz is a half-breed human man with pale skin, red scaly patches, and a lizard-like tail. He was the owner of the Goblin Pot Tavern in Amacedia, but was arrested unjustly after defending his bar from a dangerous customer. Now he is on the run and has been traveling with the Black Raven Guild ever since they broke him out of prison.

Vesper - Vesper is the Guild Master of the Black Raven Guild. She is responsible for sending Renald, Whisperclaw, Glimmer, and Ironvine into the Tower of Abell.

Blackthorn - Blackthorn is a one eyed, black furred saber. He stole Vesper's Ethereal Enchantment Scroll and had been orchestrating a series of robberies in order to host an illegal auction with all of the stolen items. He disappeared after setting a failed ambush for the Black Raven Guild in Amacedia's town hall.

Hawk - Hawk Wind is the King of all Bounty Hunters, and Glimmer's father. Not much is known about his past, but at some point he, Glimmer, and his other son Glam fell out with each other. When Glam ran away, Hawk changed, so Glimmer went after him, but that only resulted in him losing another son.

Vanhiel - Vanhiel is currently the best Bounty Hunter in the world, other than Hawk, and was also Hawk's most loyal Inner Circle member. That was until Vanhiel betrayed Hawk, staging a coup to take over the city of Denzen with the other Inner Circle members.

Spots - Spots is a Jackal that Renald and Whisperclaw met at Wolfy's Tavern who initially provided them with information about the Wind family and the inner workings of Denzen. To everyone's surprise, she turned out to be working with the Inner Circle the whole time and aided in Renald and Whisperclaw's capture.

Ash - Ash is a gray skinned senat who was sent by Spots to capture Renald and Whisperclaw during the coup in Denzen. He is also one of the Inner Circle members working alongside Vanhiel.

Sneaker - Sneaker is a mysterious Bounty Hunter who hides their real identity by wearing a dragon skull mask over their face. Sneaker is part of the Inner Circle and works closely with Vanhiel.

Eudora - Eudora is a Red and White skinned senat woman who slept with Glimmer. It was later revealed that she not only worked for Hawk, but was part of the Inner Circle and played an integral part in capturing Whisperclaw.

Lucky - Lucky is Eudora's Silverstripe Panther, a large, black fur covered creature with a silver stripe going down its back. For a monster, it seems surprisingly tame.

Fraken - Doctor Fraken is a pale, human man with a frizzy black and white afro. He has acted as the head doctor for the Wind Family for generations and is a part of the Inner Circle. For some reason, he has decided to team up with Vanhiel in order to overthrow Hawk.

Introduction

"**I** wonder..." Xyron mutters, pulling his longsword from the mutilated corpse of a 13-foot-tall goblin.

The blade pulses as it drinks deeply from the goblin's corpse, blood seeping into its thirsty steel until it overflows in crimson rivulets. Xyron manipulates the extra blood with his mind, willing it into the shape of a large, smooth orb through which he watches the chaos unfolding in Denzen. Blackthorn had done well, so well that Hawks' own trusted advisors and friends all turned on him within a single night. The promise of power can be quite compelling, can't it?

"Still keeping an eye on them?" Tiphony leaps onto Xyron's back, peering over his shoulder at the orb. "Looks like we missed all the fun, huh?"

"Eager to spill blood, as always," Xyron says with a laugh, ruffling Tiphony's messy blonde hair.

Compared to him, she looks smaller than a child. Xyron stands over 8 feet tall, easily, while Tiphony barely makes 5 feet tall. The difference in height is staggering to look at or even try to make sense of.

"Heehee." Tiphony grins from ear to ear, taking Xyron's comment as a compliment. Her fangs glistening rubies under the moonlight.

"I can understand her sentiment, I'm afraid." Bayenor kicks the head of the goblin slightly in disgust. "I thought we would be able to do a little more to help, but you ended up finishing the beast in one blow."

"Don't worry, you two; there'll be more bosses to fight. Trust me." Xyron looks over to Glam, who had been silently watching them since the group arrived at the first-floor boss room. "Besides, I had to show our new friend here what he's getting himself into."

Glam remains impassive at Xyron's words, walking past to sit on the goblin's bloody chest. With his palm pressed to the goblin's cold skin, Glam channeled a crackling blue aura. The creature's limbs jerked unnaturally, bones creaking as it let out a tortured, guttural moan.

"Xyron, what's he doing?" Tiphony asks, her curiosity piqued.

"Shhh. Just watch," Xyron replies, a wild smile spreading across his face.

As Glam's hand pulses with energy, the goblin rises to its feet behind him, its eyes glowing with the same ominous hue as the aura that revived it.

"Hooray! Hooray!" Tiphony cheers gleefully, rushing forward with outstretched arms.

"That's not a toy, Tiphony," Bayenor warns, restraining her before she can bite into the monster's leg. "Nor is it food. We're here to work, so let's maintain some professionalism."

"But I'm hungry!" Tiphony whines, licking her lips. "Just a nibble, please?"

"Control yourself," Bayenor mutters, his grip tightening.

Glam steps closer to Xyron, eyes drawn to the swirling blood in the orb. Recognition flickers in his eyes, eliciting a wider smile from Xyron. Things are getting interesting indeed.

THE INNER CIRCLE

It's a shame Xyron won't get to witness the impending confrontation between Glam and his brother. Somehow, even though they were one step behind Xyron's group in Amacedia, those four managed to lose weeks worth of ground in only a few days.

"Why are you so interested in what happens in Denzen?" Glam asks directly, bypassing any pleasantries.

"Denzen is just the stage," Xyron replies, his eyes gleaming. "The real star of the show is someone else."

Chapter 33: The Sovereign's Challenge

(Renald)

A dull pain radiates from the back of my skull as I wake to the jangle of keys and clanging metal. The last thing I remember is the stab—betrayed by Spot. She teamed up with the shirtless senat and attacked us. Wait—where's Whisperclaw?

Groggily, I survey my surroundings. A small prison cell, its walls damp and cold, holds me captive. I'm on the bottom bunk of a bunk bed, stripped of my armor, shield, and saber. Instead, I wear ragged potato sack cloth with holes for pants and a shirt. I hear rustling above. Who's there? I stand and see a small, blue-skinned snargle rubbing the sleep from his eyes. He looks like an older version of Glimmer. They must be related.

"Hmm? Finally awake," the man yawns, his voice casual. "You were in bad shape when they threw you in here. Watching your wounds close on their own was... disturbing."

"Sorry about that." I mumble, unsure why I feel the need to apologize.

"You're here for Glimmer, right?" he asks, climbing down. "Does he know he's been traveling with a vampire, or were you planning to keep that secret?"

"Who are you?" I evade his question, focusing on his identity instead.

"Really? You don't recognize me?" He finally stands before me, his gaze piercing. "What are they teaching you knights nowadays?"

"I'm not a knight."

The cell door bursts open, revealing a dark brown-furred saber, shorter but bulkier than me. A large hammer dangles from his side along with a set of rusty keys.

"Alright, you two, move it!" he roars, his voice echoing off the stone walls. "We've got a schedule to keep!"

The snargle and I exchange a brief, puzzled glance before the saber's patience snaps. He lunges, gripping us by our throats, and drags us down a long, dark corridor. The stone floor is rough beneath my bare feet, the air damp and heavy. After several twists and turns, we reach another large cell. Two bounty hunters in mismatched knight's armor guard the door. Their blood-stained gear tells of past violence.

"Hurry up and open the gate!" The saber barks. "I'm already late!"

The guards comply, unlocking the gate and sliding it open. We're hurled into the cell like ragdolls, crashing into cold metal bars. The air is thick with the damp stench of sweat and blood. The gate clangs shut behind us.

"Hahaha!" The saber's laughter echoes as he walks away. "See you in the arena! Can't wait for your performance..hahahaha!"

I sigh. What does he mean, see you in the arena? I turn around to see what I slammed into and, as if to answer my question, I see another gate leading into a massive colosseum.

"Renald?" I hear a very familiar voice come from the shadows in the cell.

THE INNER CIRCLE

I whip back around, looking for the owner of the voice. To my surprise, I see Glimmer emerge from the darkness, doing his best to hold up a barely conscious Whisperclaw. I almost rush to them, but seeing Whisperclaw battered and bruised makes my hands clench into fists. She is clutching her ribs with a pained expression on her face. Blood trickles from an open gash on her forehead. Her normally smooth and shiny fur is covered in dirt and matted with dried blood. Glimmer looks slightly better than Whisperclaw. I don't see any visible wounds, but, by how messed up his shirt is, I can tell he's been in a recent fight of some sort.

"You're... you're ok?" Glimmer asks, looking kind of confused, "When I saw them dragging you in yesterday, I thought you were dead."

"Almost, but not quite." My voice tightens with restrained fury. "Where are we?"

"We're in one of the holding cells underneath the arena." The snargle man who was dragged here with me answers, making his way over to us. "We're as good as dead in here."

"Dad?" Glimmer's eyes go wide with recognition at the sight of the man. "Dad! I thought Vanhiel and the others killed you."

"Wait, you're..." All of the anger that I've been holding back suddenly bursts.

I feel the very air around me begin to shiver, and the little light shining into the holding cell begins to slowly dissipate. I'm on him before I know it, my hand around his throat, slamming him against the wall. Everything in me screams to crush it, to end him.

"You're the reason we're in this mess! You!" I feel a tingly sensation in my gums, and my senses sharpen. "You're the reason Whisper's hurt! I should kill you right now! Leave you dead where you stand!"

My vision blurs with red rage. Dark, violent thoughts crowd my mind—each more brutal than the last. He doesn't deserve to live. Scum like him deserve nothing more than to return to the void.

"Renald!" Glimmer's unusually stern voice pulls me back into the present. "I know how you feel, but you can't. He's still my dad."

I glare into the eyes of the snargle, gasping for air. It would be so easy to end him—one twist, one snap. But something holds me back—a sliver of restraint I don't understand. Maybe it's Glimmer. Maybe it's something else. I suck my teeth and release my grip. The man slides down the wall and starts coughing until he can breathe again.

"T-thank you, son." I hear Glimmer's dad mutter through deep breaths.

"I didn't do it for you." Glimmer stares at his father with absolutely no emotions whatsoever. "I did it for mom."

Then, Glimmer slowly places Whisperclaw face down on the cell floor. I see a huge, open cut going down her back. Who would do this? Spot, that bitch. If I had never trusted her to begin with, this wouldn't have happened.

"She needs a doctor." Glimmer says worriedly. "Where's Ironvine and the others at? If we can get him to her, he can save her."

"I don't know." I lower my voice to a whisper. "They went to secure us a way out of the city, but I haven't heard anything since we separated."

"If they are trying to use some kind of magic, it's pointless in here." Glimmer's dad tries to chime in. "We're in an anti-magic prison."

"We didn't ask you." I glare at the man, trying to kill him with my eyes.

"Renald, please. Believe me when I say that I hate him a thousand times more than you do, but we need his help." I feel Glimmer's hand fall onto my shoulder. "He built this entire city, so he's our best bet if we're going to get out of here alive."

"I wish that were true." I look back at Glimmer's father. "Vanhiel plans to take the sovereign's challenge—the old way of seizing power without breaking the law. One-on-one combat, no rules."

"Excuse me, but not all of us are familiar with Bounty Hunter laws." I scoff at him. "What exactly is this 'Sovereign's Challenge' you're talking about?"

"It's-" Glimmer pauses to think for a moment.

"You both are impossible, especially you Glimmer." Glimmer's father begins to reprimand him. "Any Fourth Ring member can challenge me—or any king—for the throne. A one-on-one fight to the death. No rules."

"You used to be the king, right?" I ask. "So why can't you just beat Vanhiel and take back over?"

"Because I'm not as young as I used to be." Glimmer's dad looks away in shame. "My powers have been fading ever since I had my first son."

"Dad…" Glimmer suddenly has a sad expression on his face. "I had no clue. Does mom know?"

"I thought nobody did, but I guess Vanhiel started to catch on after I never chased after you and Glam." Glimmer's dad sighs.

I think I realize what's happening. Glimmer's father must have never told him about what he was going through. This whole time, he was suffering alone. For now, I think I'll just stay quiet. I was never good with handling mushy family stuff anyway.

"You knew this was going to happen, didn't you?" Glimmer walks over and sits down next to his dad. "That's why you were pushing me and Glam so hard."

"I never wanted to hurt either of you." Glimmer's dad clenches his fists. "I just needed to make sure that you both would be strong enough for when this day came."

"Dad…" Glimmer places a hand on his dad's shoulder. "I-"

He never gets to finish his statement. The gate leading into the colosseum rattles open, pouring light into the dark cell. Two figures in bloody knight armor, who I assume to be more bounty hunters, enter the cell slowly. One of them is holding a large pole with a wire hoop attached at the end, something that I've seen tamers use for handling dangerous beasts. Without saying a single word to any of us, they march over to where Glimmer and his father are sitting and place the hoop gently around Glimmer's dad's neck. In a split second, the hoop snaps shut, and the two figures start to drag him out of the cell and back out into the colosseum.

THE INNER CIRCLE

"Dad!" Glimmer screams, tears of anger leaking from his pleading eyes, "You have to win! You can beat him! I know you can!"

Boom! I barely catch Glimmer before he slams into the gate, his screams echoing off the stone walls. It's over—his father is gone. The challenge has begun—and all we can do is watch.

Chapter 34: All You Have To Do

(Whisperclaw)

I'm standing among my brothers-in-arms. We're all at attention, the rain unrelenting as we face the large balcony. Each of us wears the same uniform: black armor with three red claw marks slashed across the chest, paired with matching gauntlets and boots. Commander Shadewind stands above us, flanked by Church of Azia members. We are the Wardogs, the newest unit in the Keyonian Military.

A blink, and the rain is no longer there. Now I'm crouched on a massive tree branch, surrounded by oversized leaves that blot out the sky. Glintwax and Stonehedge, my fellow Wardogs, squat on nearby branches. Below us, a caravan of five carts passes slowly. Each cart is drawn by large, furred beasts with antlers, guarded by Elenonian Royal Guards clad in star-patterned cloaks. Silver blades hang from their horses' sides. A sharp whistle cuts through the air—the caravan halts. I know they've hit our blockade—a tree we felled on the road less than an hour ago. Glintwax, Stonehedge, and I nod to each other before leaping from our perches. I shadowstep into the center cart and slit the King of Elenona's throat before he can react. Just as swiftly as I entered, I shadowstepped out, reappearing beside my comrades who stand amid the slaughtered guards. Blood pools on the dirt like rainwater. A door creaks open, and

19

a small green-eyed girl with blue hair peers out of one of the carts.

Once again, everything shifts. Now, I'm standing on a stage at a party full of noble Keyonian families. I recognize a few faces, but that doesn't matter—they all recognize me. Commander Shadewind approaches with a golden medal in his paw, pinning it to my formal uniform. In the crowd, I see Brownclaw raise a glass silently. His smirk causes my face to flush with warmth. It'll be a year before he asks me out. Two before he proposes.

"Dad!"

I'm jolted awake by Glimmer's scream. My eyes snap open, and I lurch up, wincing as pain shoots down my spine.

"Hey! Hey..." Renald's voice is steady as he eases me back down. "Don't move. You're badly injured."

Glimmer clings to the bars of the metal gate, his blue face streaked with tears. He's fixated on another snargle, far across a massive colosseum. A blast of blue energy flashes, slamming into the snargle, who slides back before batting the energy away with his bare hands. The crowd roars.

"What's happening?" I ask, grabbing Renald's wrist. "Where are we? What happened to Ironvine? Why is Glimmer crying?"

Renald glances toward the gate, a flicker of sadness in his otherwise stoic eyes. Then, with a resigned sigh, his expression hardens. Renald leans in, his voice low but insistent.

"How do you shadowstep?"

"What? That's a national secret; you think I would just tell you something like that?" I bristle, torn between loyalty and instinct. Renald's question feels like a betrayal, yet there's something in the way he asks, a quiet desperation, that makes me pause.

"I don't have time to explain." Renald's tone sharpens with urgency. "Just tell me—do you use magic to do it?"

"N-no." I stammer, caught off-guard by my honesty. "We're guildmates, but I really shouldn't tell you this."

"Good." Renald grins. "The prison's antimagic defenses can't stop you then. With your injuries, how many times can you do it? "

"Once. Maybe," I say. "To be honest, that'll probably push me to my limit."

Renald pulls his arm free and marches over to Glimmer, ripping him away from the gate. Glimmer struggles, desperate to watch the fight.

"Let me go! I have to save him! I can't just stand here."

"And do what?" Renald cuts him off, stern but calm. "What will watching accomplish?"

"I don't know!" Glimmer shouts, eyes wide with panic. "But I have to do something! I can't just sit here and wait for Vanhiel to kill him! He's my dad, Renald!"

"I know." Renald pulls Glimmer into a tight hug. "However, freaking out won't save him."

Glimmer thrashes, a desperate, hopeless fight—until his strength crumbles, leaving him sobbing in Renald's arms. Renald holds firm, a rock he can lean on. I'm stunned—I've never seen Renald act like this before. After a while, Glimmer's tears subside. Renald gently releases him and crouches down so Glimmer won't have to look up.

"Do you want your father saved?" Renald's voice is steady, but beneath it, I hear an urgency that's new, almost pleading.

As if uncertain of his own response, Glimmer nods slowly. "Then ask."

"Please..." Glimmer's voice is soft.

"Huh? What was that?" Renald cups a hand to his ear.

"Please help me save my father! " Glimmer shouts, rage mixing with the remnants of his tears.

"That's all you had to say!" Renald grins, his golden eyes blazing. "Team, I'm sorry if I haven't been the best leader, but I need you now. One last time!"

"What's the plan, wise leader?" I wince through the pain but laugh.

"We're shadowstepping into the colosseum," Renald says, as if it's the simplest thing in the world—though we all know it isn't. "Leave the rest to me."

Glimmer nods in agreement, walking over to where I'm lying. Renald grabs one of my paws and touches Glimmer's shoulder. Glimmer grabs my other paw.

"Glimmer," Renald commands, "once we're there, protect Whisperclaw with your life. Leave the rest to me."

"Uh..." I interject. "We have no weapons."

"Trust me." The already shady cell darkens even more as Renald answers, "We have all the weapons we need."

Renald's pupils narrow to predatory slits, gleaming in the dim light. His canines extend with an audible click. As his wings unfurl with a leathery rasp, the air around him thickens, charged with the primal energy of a beast about to strike. His barbed tail flicks around behind him in all directions. Renald doesn't need to say anything more. From here, I just have to trust him.

"Alright!" I yell. "Hold on tight!"

THE INNER CIRCLE

I was already lying in the darkest section of the cell, so all I have to do is let the darkness take me. I slip into it, pulling Renald and Glimmer with me. We fall backward, down into the abyss. All we can do now is trust each other, no hesitating.

Chapter 35: Power of The Wind

(Ironvine)

"Why aren't they working? They should have been working by now, right?"

Liaz taps his foot in apparent lack of patience. His tail sways back and forth while he, Goldenclaw, and I stand in a circle. Each of us clutches a small, glowing, white feather. Three of the teleportation feathers we'd discovered inside the chest in the first room of the dungeon King led us to. Now we only have one problem, getting them to work.

"You said we just had to picture the person we're trying to teleport to, but that doesn't seem to work." I say, relaxing my arm. "Let's take a break for a minute. I feel like we've been trying to do this for hours now."

"That's because we have-" Liaz presses his eyes shut in an attempt to concentrate until he gives up and tosses his feather back into the chest. "You know what? Damn it! I'm sick of messing with this stupid feather!"

"It has to be some kind of magical disturbance on their end." Goldenclaw plops down, his normally pristine mane drenched in sweat.

"What do we do now?" I ask, sitting next to him crossed legged. "Even focusing on Glimmer didn't work."

"Something isn't right. I can smell it!" Liaz sits down as well, completing an unintentional triangle. "Why couldn't we teleport to Glimmer? His dad owns the place, right?"

Nobody says anything. There are so many questions unanswered right now. I look at Liaz and Goldenclaw, who both appear just as unsure as myself. Goldenclaw looks up at me while pondering deeply. He laughs.

"Ironvine, your-bwah! Ha, ha, ha!"

I'm shocked at this sudden burst of laughter. Liaz looks up at me and laughs too.

"Ha,ha,ha,ha! Why is your skin like that?" He bellows."Your skin is-it's pink! Ha, ha, ha, ha!"

"What is wrong with both of you? If you can laugh, you've got the energy to keep trying!" I bare my fangs at both of them. "Our friends could be in danger right now."

"No, you're right, you're right, but-I can't take you seriously when you're pink!" They both burst out laughing again at Goldenclaw's comment.

I really don't get comedy. My fur changes color depending on my mood. It happens to all Chim-Chis. Standing up, I grab three feathers out of the box and shove one into each of their hands.

"Focus!" I say, shutting my eyes.

They continue to laugh but I ignore them, trying to think about Glimmer's face. He's short, only coming up to my stomach area. He has shiny blue skin and white hair, which sometimes glows at night. His eyes are sparkly dark black, like a dark pond. Suddenly, laughter grows into roars all around me, getting louder and louder until suddenly, they stop.

THE INNER CIRCLE

The roars become gasps. I feel the wind whipping across my face, prompting me to finally open my eyes. I'm falling. I fully realize what's happening before I slam into the ground. Thankfully, I can cover my body in Celestria's energy. My bones are being shattered into pieces by the impact of the crash, but I can feel all damage being reversed instantly as a result of the green aura that surrounds me.

A small crater surrounds me, and I pause for a moment to take a deep breath. The first thing I notice is that the sun is very bright. Also, I'm surrounded by rich golden sand. I'm not in the dungeon anymore, but that would mean I should be with Glimmer right now. I stand up and dust myself off. Clutching my recently acquired double-sided stone sword, I march out of the crater.

"Ironvine lookout!" I instinctively roll to the left, choosing not to focus on who spoke.

I slide backwards and slam into something. I whip around and see a massive stone wall. I finally get a second to look at my surroundings and notice I'm in the middle of a massive colosseum. I see a yellow scaled draken, with sky blue eyes and a wide brimmed hat on, holding a mana pistol pointed in my direction.

I recognize this man instantly. It's the bounty hunter who snatched Glimmer and teleported away. I feel myself boil with anger. I charge at the man. He fires off two shots that slam through my armor, but Celestria's energy heals the wounds. I quickly close the distance between us and try to slice him in half with my sword. He jumps backwards, twirling in the air and slinging a mana shotgun into my face. I twirl the sword around and knock the shotgun away before it fires. Now we're standing face to face. The crowd around us applauds and shouts in delight.

"Where the fuck did you come from?" He snarls, blue electricity crackling around in his mouth.

"Forgot about me?" I see a snargle who looks like Glimer appear in the blink of an eye.

Just as fast, he punches the draken in the face, sending him flying across the colosseum. I watch in awe as the draken plants both his feet into the ground to slow the momentum. He tosses his guns and slams his claws into the sand. I blink and the snargle is gone. At the same time the draken sends ten massive electricity waves shaped like dragons in my direction. They swim through the sand, turning it into molten lava and glass. I close my eyes and brace for impact.

"I got you!" I feel something scooping me up off the ground.

My eyes fly open and I see that Renald has picked me up and is flying with me towards Glimmer and Whisperclaw in the arena shade. Behind us, the electricity wave dragons crash into the colosseum wall. The draken looks at us for a second and pays for it by getting sucker punched away again by the snargle.

"Quick! You gotta heal Whisperclaw and Glimmer so we can get the hell out of here!" Renald yells landing and quickly placing me down.

I don't even have time to ask about the situation before Renald takes off into the sky. He then returns to the ongoing battle between the snargle and the draken. I touch Whisperclaw's unconscious forehead and Glimmer's shoulder. I envision Celestria's energy spreading from my body and onto the others.

THE INNER CIRCLE

The green cloak around me follows my mind's orders and covers Glimmer and Whisperclaw, healing all their wounds. A multitude of thoughts shroud my mind, filled with the different ways they could have ended up like this.

"Well this is a fascinating turn of events! It looks like we have some extra competitors joining in on the fun!"

My eyes snap to the sky where I see a dull colored, brown skinned snargle wearing a suit hovering above us. He has on a pair of glasses with blacked-out lenses and holds his finger up to his mouth as he yells into it like a microphone.

"Should we even up this battle a little?" He directs the question to the crowd, which roars in response. "Alright! Ash! Sneaker! Eudora! Fraken! Come out!"

The snargle points his finger towards the far left side of the colosseum stands. At the exact moment he finishes pointing, I see three figures I don't recognize leaping down from the top of the wall. The first to land is a shirtless, gray skinned senat with a long sword on his back. Next to him, a figure with their face completely covered by a dragon skull mask lands. They are wearing a black jacket with the hood thrown over their head and wielding a sword with a spike encrusted blade. On the right of the shirtless senat, a senat woman with red skin covered in white patches lands and throws out a small crystal. The crystal explodes in a small blast of fire and an all black panther with a silver stripe down its back appears in its place.

"Stand back everyone!" The snargle man hovering above us shouts.

Standing on the top of the wall that the other figures dropped down from, I see the outline of a human man. The sun shines directly behind him, covering his entire body in darkness while everything around him is illuminated. He stabs something into his neck and leaps down from the wall. He slams his feet into the ground, causing the sand beneath him to explode all around, covering the four.

"Ironvine..." I hear Whisperclaw regaining consciousness behind me, "...these people, they're dangerous."

"Glimmer, which one hurt you and Whisperclaw?" I ask, ignoring Whisperclaw's statement.

"Ironvine, I'm serious!" My eyes widen at the fear in Whisperclaw's voice. "They beat me and Renald like it was nothing."

"They even beat Ren?" I ask, shocked.

As if to answer my question, the sand screen dissipates and I see Renald charging straight towards the gray skinned senat.

"You!" He roars. "I've got unfinished business with you!"

Renald punches the senat, who counters with his own. Their fists collide in mid air and both of them are thrown backwards. Renald does a backflip into a slight glide back onto the ground. The senat stands his ground and slides backwards with both feet firmly planted in the sand.

"Tsk." The senat sucks his teeth. "I told Hiel we should've killed them when we had the chance."

Boom! There's another explosion of electricity and sand that shakes the entire colosseum and cuts the tension in the air. Out of the smoke, the snargle from earlier barrels down into the sand in front of us. The draken who took Glimmer gets flung out of the smoke and across from us, landing in front of the other four figures.

"What a spectacular battle folks! Who knew that our very own Vanhiel would ever be able to keep up with the legendary Hawk Wind?" The announcer calls out to the crowd.

The crowd erupts at the mention of Vanhiel's name but groans when Hawk Wind comes up. It doesn't seem like they care about him too much.

"Vanhiel! It's over!" The snargle, who I'm assuming is Hawk Wind, cries out. "You can't beat me, and you know it."

"We'll see about that." The draken, Vanhiel, laughs. "You think just because you had some kids interrupt the challenge you'll win? You've gotten slow, old man."

"Enough!" Hawk shouts in anger. "You've done nothing but destroy my kingdom and disgrace my name and my family! Now I will show you why your ancestors crowned me king all those years ago! I'll show you why your family has always bowed to me and mine!"

In rage, Vanhiel screams with anger, looking pissed off. He points his index finger at Hawk like a gun, then presses his thumb down like he pulled the trigger. A massive Mana blast fires from his fingertip, and it slams straight into Hawk. Hawk doesn't budge. The blast explodes on contact and kicks up another sand screen. When the sand clears, however, Hawk is not alone anymore. Instead, he stands behind a massive, undead dragon. It is almost completely bones now, with most of its remaining flesh being a sickly purple color and covered in abscess pockets.

Hawk shouts, "This is the Wind Family's power!"

Chapter 36: Not Safe Out There

(Glimmer)

I'm literally shaking. I feel absolutely powerless right now. I don't have my flute so I can't summon any of my illusions. My father is fighting one of the most powerful bounty hunters in history, and I can't help. Even Ironvine is fighting, but all I can do is watch.

"Don't worry Glimmer." I feel Whisperclaw push down on my shoulder, using it as support to stand to her feet. "We'll save your dad. Try to find a way to get our stuff back. That's the most effective way to help us right now."

She pats my shoulder and steps into my shadow. Then she smirks at me and nods. I realize what she's doing when it's too late. I feel my feet slip out from underneath me and I spiral downwards, through my own shadow. Then I am spit out, sliding across a cobblestone road in an abandoned alleyway. I scramble to my feet and look around quickly. Whisperclaw must have shadow-stepped me outside the colosseum. I get it. With me out of the way the others won't have to worry about my safety. They can focus on winning all out and beating Vanhiel and the rest of the Inner Circle.

"Psst..." I think I hear someone so I look over my shoulder and see three young boys looking around the corner at me. "..hey you! Come on over for a second."

All three of them motion for me to move towards them. Oddly enough, they are completely in sync with each other. They don't seem dangerous, if anything they seem like more genuine people than anyone I've met since entering the tower. The loading dock behind me is completely deserted, other than a few closed boxes and a port full of at least 12 small ships. I look back at the three boys and point to myself, trying to make sure they are talking to me.

"Yes, you!" The boy in the middle, who looks the eldest of the group, says with a frown. "Hurry up before one of the bad guys comes and catches you!"

I slowly walk over to the trio. They look like brothers. Each of them has scruffy, orangish red hair, deeply tanned skin, dark brown eyes, and freckles on their cheeks. They wear different colored fishing hats that seem old and worn down. The one who called out to me appears to be the oldest and is wearing a stained red cloth as a shirt. He is taller than all the others and even I have to look up to avoid staring at his chest. They open up a makeshift wooden door that barely fits into the doorway and motion for me to enter. I glance around outside hesitantly, but it looks like a ghost town, the exact opposite of yesterday. I sigh, then walk through the doorway and into the building.

The inside is dark and cool, with a single lamp sitting on a table surrounded by four wooden chairs, dimly lighting what seems to be a tiny kitchen. A small and porcelain-like human woman, small by human standards anyway, stirs a giant silver pot of chili. She has graying, long and curly red hair and deep blue eyes. She has a red and white checkered apron on and looks at me with surprise, then pity.

THE INNER CIRCLE

"Mars, who is it?" A man's voice shouts from a nearby hall-way. "If it's not the boys, tell them to go away. I need to finish preparations!"

"I think you should see this Shane! I think you would be happy!" The woman shouts back, changing her face to one of irritation.

"Ah, I'm sorry to intrude but those boys-" Right on cue the trio walks in behind me and plops down at the table. "Well, you see they-"

"Don't worry Glimmer, I already know." The woman stir-ring the pot smiles at me softly, but her eyes are full of sorrow. "I'm sorry about your father's situation."

"Wait, how do you know my-"

"Bless the spirits of the wind and seas!" My question is rudely interrupted by a very toned and dark skinned man who enters the kitchen from beyond the hallway. "Just how lucky can we get in one day, Mars?"

"I already told you, leave me and the boys out of this." The woman, Mars, tells the man. "How could you have your own sons running around out there? Think Shane! What if one of them got spotted? Couldn't you have sent one of those knights you have hiding in our bedroom?"

"I'm-" The man pauses, his face showing deep thought and worry, before speaking again. "I'm sorry. You're right. But all of that's over now, we've got everything we need."

"Ok, I really don't mean to be rude but can somebody tell me what's happening?" I ask, getting fed up with being ignored. "Who are you people and what do you want from me?"

"We wanna know what's happening too!" One of the trio, who looks the smallest and youngest of the bunch, pouts from his seat at the table. "You always leave us out of the good stuff."

"Ahh, I know little shark." Shane scoops up the boy into his arms. "I promise that one day, you and all of your brothers will know everything."

"Alright, I don't have time for this." I go for the door, my patience breaking. "Good luck with whatever you have planned. I've got more serious things to do."

Right as I swing the door open and am about to leave, I feel a hand grab my shoulder gently. It's Mars, looking at me softly and shaking her head slowly.

"Please. It's not safe out there for anyone right now." She says with a soft voice. "Vanhiel has bounty hunters from the Fourth Ring patrolling the streets. They're capturing anyone they see, and they will probably kill you on the spot. Your face is easily recognizable in this city."

I look across the street for a brief moment before deciding to hear these people out. They seem like they want to help, and more than that they seem like they know something significant. Why else would they be glad to see me of all people? I can't even use magic right now.

"I'm so sorry for making you wait, your highness. Please forgive an old fisherman." The man, Shane, shifts his wife to the side and sticks his hand out towards me as if for a handshake. "I'm Shane Coshimare, of the Coshimare Fishing Company. It's a pleasure to meet you."

"There's no need to call me 'your highness.'" I reply and shut the front door and fully turn to look Shane in the eyes. "Now, what do you want from me?"

"Straight to the point, huh?" Shane looks taken aback for a second but quickly recomposes himself, relaxing his hand. "Let's find someplace more private to talk, if you don't mind."

"Sure." I shrug. "I get it, you don't want your kids hearing whatever it is."

"Bango. Hit the nail on the head." Shane chuckles and leads me down the hall and to a closed door.

It takes him a few moments to pull out the key and unlock it before he can swing the door open. He motions for me to enter and I hesitate briefly. I suck up my nerves and step into the shadowy interior. The room is full of at least 20 knights wearing the Sellsword Guild crest on their chest plates. I freeze. They set me up. One of the knights, with three embellished blue and white striped feathers tapered at the top of his helm, stands quickly to his feet and points at me. I go for the door. I slam into Shane's chest, who catches me by the arms before I fall backwards.

"Woah there, young prince! It's alright!" He says. "These people can help you! Please, give them a chance!"

"No! These people tried to kill me and my friends!" I shout.

I try to headbutt Shane in the face, but he dodges it. Then he slips behind me, spins me around, and softly pushes me back into the room. All the other knights are standing now, glaring at me. One in particular, who has his helmet off revealing the face of a dark skinned, young human man with glasses on, holds up a bounty poster. It has a rough sketch of my face and a massive bounty of 100,000 Sapphires. He smirks and pushes up his glasses before speaking.

"I'm sorry, but we have a bounty out for this one and his 'friends.'"

Chapter 37: Cut Loose

(Renald)

I fly backwards as fast as I can, scooping up Whisperclaw into my arms and soaring far into the sky. Beneath us, green smoke falls heavily from the undead dragon's maw. It quickly fills up the opposite side of the arena from us, where Vanhiel and the other inner circle members are. Vanhiel cuts through the smoke using a lightning sword, dashing towards Glimmer's father. The dragon snaps his mouth shut and I see a spark fly off of its sharp teeth as they collide together.

I turn my back on the coliseum and pull Whisperclaw into my chest, bracing for impact. The sheer force of the explosion slings me forward. The sound echoes loudly in my ears and I feel a burning sensation in my right wing. The burning is followed by an intense pain which causes me to instinctively fold it. The next thing I know, we're hurtling towards the stands below us. I twist in midair, falling onto my back so Whisperclaw won't be hurt. I feel something in my back snap and my body crashes through the stands. Dust and debris kick up around us, pieces of wood and metal splintering off in different directions. Everything hurts from my hips to my neck. To make matters more difficult, I can't feel my legs anymore.

"Shit! You idiot!" Whisperclaw yells, scrambling off me and onto her feet. "You didn't have to do that, I could have shadow stepped away! You wasted so much time saving me for that-"

"Whisperclaw, I think my back is broken." I interrupt her with a gasp of pain.

"Oh no. Ironvine!" She looks around hysterically. "We need Ironvine! You need to wait right here. I'll-I'll-"

I can see tears beginning to pool around the bottom of her eyes. She quickly attempts to wipe them away. It's probably all the debris in the air, or maybe she's crying? That's right, I think to myself. She doesn't know.

"Calm down. I'll heal in a minute, but I need some help getting to my feet." I say calmly, trying to convey my emotions to Whisperclaw through my voice. "Hurry, before the debris clears. We don't want to have other bounty hunters trying to-"

All of the debris and dust disperse in an instant and the announcer, a brown skinned snargle, hovers directly above our small crater. He flicks his hand to the side and I see the dust and debris from earlier shoot out of the tips of his fingers and out of the colosseum. Surrounding the edge of the crater, the bounty hunters who have been watching us fight are now looking at Whisperclaw and I. All of them have different weapons in their hands, from knives and swords to mana pistols and rifles. This is bad. I can feel it.

"What a spectacular evasive maneuver folks!" The announcer shouts as loud as possible, his voice echoing throughout the entire coliseum. "It's too bad that they landed beyond the coliseum, isn't that right? If you didn't know, any competitor with a bounty on them is free to be captured or killed if they venture out of the arena! So, have at it boys!"

THE INNER CIRCLE

I feel another snap in my back and all the feeling returns to my legs. In a single motion, I'm back on my feet, shoving Whisperclaw behind me just as a mana bullet fires past both our heads. One of the bounty hunters rushes us with an axe, but I slip under it and clothesline him. I put all my strength into flinging him back out of the crater and he flies into the crowd. I could feel my arm cracking through his ribs. I smile just a little.

"Whisper, get out of here! Get back and help Ironvine and Glimmer's Dad!" I shout. "Now! I've got things covered up here."

"R-right!" I hear her respond and then she falls silent.

My grin grows even wider. Now that she's no longer here, I can actually unwind a little. Sorry Ironvine, I apologize in my head. It looks like I'm about to kill somebody again. I let out a roar, finally allowing all of my pent up anger to burst to the surface. All of my senses are once again heightened and I can feel my bloodlust taking control. For the first time since my fight with Carcavella almost a year ago, I let loose.

My senses are heightened. I can hear the heartbeats of all the bounty hunters around me. I can smell their fear. I close my eyes, taking in the brief moment of tranquility these people have before they meet Abell in the afterlife. My rage has fully engulfed me. I feel it spreading over my entire body, taking over my motor functions. My body has started acting independently.

"What are we waiting for?" I clear the distance between myself and my target, who tried to shoot Whisperclaw mere moments ago, in a fraction of a second. "Holy-"

I stomp my foot into his face, cutting him off mid-sentence and sending him flying into others around him. Within seconds, my vision fills with blood. Somebody throws a dagger, which my body instinctively slips past. I charge towards them, slashing through everyone in my way with newly formed blood claws. Their blood to be exact.

I reach for the culprit and stab my claws into their stomach, raising them up into the air and letting their blood rain down on me. It smells sour. This person didn't deserve to live, their blood says it. I feel my body backwards, dodging a mana bullet that slams into someone behind me.

Now I'm lashing out at everything that moves. The blood I drank a second ago boosted my adrenaline. All I see around me is blood and screams of horror. Everyone's blood is tainted. Everyone deserves death. Nobody among them shall survive my wraith.

Then the screaming stops. I feel myself taking back control, my rage dying out. The red that obscured my vision gradually fades away. I'm breathing heavily. Everything hurts and I feel sick at the core of my stomach. I can smell the blood fuming from the mass of dead bodies before I see them.

My vision returns and now I see them. I am surrounded by death everywhere I look. Hundreds, maybe even thousands of bounty hunters lay dead around me. I feel something slimy in my hand and toss it away in disgust. It's a small brown hand. I look beneath me and see the announcer's mutilated corpse.

I scramble backwards, my breathing picking up speed. Oh no, I'm starting to panic. I did it again. Why? Why? Why? Why? I had to! I had to do it! It was me or them! My chest feels tight. I'm gasping for breath, but I can't get enough. My ears are filled with a sharp ringing. I can see her staring at me, amid smoke in the East River District.

"Carcavella I'm sorry!" I yell, gripping my blood saber tightly.

She doesn't respond. She walks towards me slowly, completely controlled by her Ascent Core. The all-white living armor shines perfectly as if all the fighting so far gave it a much needed polish. As for mine, I cannot judge, I have the same problem. Instead of all white, mine is all red.

I can smell the thousands of dead bodies beneath the rubble, right underneath our feet. I don't understand. Things are so different now than when we were living with General Black. Carcavella has lost all sense of reason. She just wants to watch the world burn. I feel my Ascent Core pulsing against my skin. It's trying to comfort me.

I rush into Carcavella, lashing out with everything that I have. She effortlessly dodges every attack. I try to kick but she sticks her hand out and stops me. She laughs. A manic laugh unlike any I've heard before.

"It seems like you don't understand anything, don't you?" she shrills. "I never needed you! Not then and especially not now! I'm strong enough to make my own decisions and choose Renald! I choose chaos!"

The sounds of heavy, rapidly approaching footsteps fill the air. Carcavella releases me and kicks me into a pile of debris that used to be a small shop. Then she walks away.

"Don't worry, I'll play with you again soon..." She laughs. The flames around us flare up then the entire vision disperses.

"Hahaha!" The shirtless gray-skinned senat claps enthusiastically. "I'll tell you what! You sir, can fight your ass off!"

For a moment, I think I see Carcavella walking towards me, but when I blink it's just him. I suck my teeth, not this guy again.

He's smiling like a madman. "You're a Black, aren't you?"

I pick up a simple looking short sword off the ground. I feel the weight. A little heavier than my saber but I can make do for now.

"Not gonna answer huh?" The senat is still talking. "Fine. I'll beat it out of you then."

Without saying anything more, we lunge at each other.

Chapter 38: Déjà Vu

(Whisperclaw)

I emerge from the coliseum shadows. Smoke surrounds me. Ash rains down from the sky. I can hear screams from the stands. However, all of the kicked up sand and smoke from the explosion prevents me from seeing anything.

I see a large form barrelling through the smoke, coming towards me. I run towards it and slide on my knees, narrowly avoiding the massive, boney dragon's tail swinging over me. As the tail flies over my head, the smoke disperses momentarily. For a brief second I can see Ironvine dodging a punch from Fraken and smacking him away with the flat part of his recently acquired double-sided stone sword.

Suddenly, two figures appear on either side of him and smoke covers them again. I feel a burning sensation in my lungs. I've inhaled too much smoke, but I don't know where else to go. Smoke is everywhere. I cover my mouth, coughing up the fumes around me. The entire ground trembles. I see a flash of blue light and look up. Falling down, right on top of me, is the body of the undead dragon Glimmer's dad summoned.

Quickly, I use the ever growing shadow cast by the falling dragon and allow myself to be swallowed by the darkness. I am spit out directly in front of the holding cell Glimmer, Renald, and I were in before. Across the coliseum, I see the massive dragon slam into the ground and completely disperse the smoke in the air. I'm looking for a way to help, but the forces in this battle seem completely out of my league.

"Hawk! Stop hiding behind this beast and fight me!" I hear Vanhiel screaming, his clothing burned and sliced. "Hawk!"

"You're going to make an outstanding servant." I see Glimmer's dad appear behind Vanhiel in a flash, faster than my eyes can blink.

He smirks and throws a right hook into Vanhiel's head. There is a loud crack and Vanhiel flies across the coliseum and slams into the wall. Dust, sand, and debris fly everywhere as he crashes through, putting a hole in it. He has to be dead after that, I think to myself. However, to my absolute horror, Vanhiel walks out of the wall with nothing but scuff marks on his yellow scales. Blue electricity crackles around him and he spits out a blood-covered tooth. He looks pissed.

"Awe! Look at this, Lucky!" a familiar voice says. "It's Whispershade!"

Leaping over the, now unmoving, body of the undead dragon is Eudora riding on the back of her pet panther. I step back cautiously. The last time we fought, those two and that crazy human man named Fraken almost killed me. Out of the corner of my eye, I see Renald slowly standing to his feet in front of the gray, shirtless senat. This whole situation gives me déjà vu. No, I shake away my fear. This time I'll beat them.

"For the last time..." I stare Eudora down, unsheathing my claws. "My name is Whisperclaw!"

"I see your attitude hasn't changed at all." Eudora hops down from Lucky's back and removes her khopesh from her side. "I wouldn't worry about it though dear, I'll fix it for you."

Lucky growls at me, likely remembering how I cut his stomach open. I laugh a little inside. That's what you deserve for trying to eat me, I think. Eudora and Lucky walk away from each other, circling me slowly. No matter how I look at it, these are losing odds. I'm in a two-vs-one fight here.

"Fuck it." Right as the words leave my lips and I move to charge Eudora on my right, I hear a loud series of gunshots fire off in rapid succession.

I duck, but it quickly becomes apparent that the shots weren't meant for me. I see Lucky take a staggered step forward, blood pouring from the three newly opened gunshot wounds on his side. My eyes dart from side to side, trying to find the shooter. That's when I see him. Liaz, with both pistols drawn, stands between me and Ironvine fighting Fraken. He looks serious, more serious than I've ever seen him before.

"There." He smirks at me. "That should even things up for you, right?"

"Liaz!" I can't help but smile.

"You-" My eyes snap back to Eudora who, for the first time since I met her, has a shocked expression on her face. "You shot Lucky! I'll kill you for this!"

Eudora rushes past me, heading straight for Liaz. I frantically attempt to leap onto her, but miss as she zooms by. In a matter of seconds, she's already closed the distance between Liaz and herself. She tries to slash across his chest but Liaz calmly leans back, dodging the attempted attack. Her back is turned to me now and I take full advantage of it. I stand up on all fours and run towards Eudora at full speed. She's so focused on attacking Liaz that she doesn't even turn around to look at me. I leap on her back and stab my claws into the holes in her armor, which are meant for her wings.

"You're supposed to fight me, remember?" I whisper confidently into her ear.

"Arghh!!" Eudora responds in pain, blood pouring from her wing joints. "Get off me you bitch!"

Liaz's eyes glow with fury at Eudora's slander. He jumps into the air and plants the bottom of both his boots into her chest, knocking Eudora off balance. We fall backwards and I lean back to make her fall faster. I feel my feet touch the sand and use the remaining momentum to throw Eudora over myself. I slam her onto her neck. I hear something inside her crack and I let her go, scrambling back to my bare feet.

"Don't talk to her like that again." Liaz snarls at Eudora, flames flickering inside his mouth.

A severely wounded Lucky leaps over her limp body, blocking us from reaching her. I don't care anymore, the fight is over. Lucky is bleeding out and can barely stand and I assume Eudora's neck has snapped. If she isn't dead, she'll be paralyzed for the rest of her life.

"Let's move Liaz, we're done here." I say, turning away from the pair and towards the battle unfolding between Ironvine and Fraken. "I'm glad you showed up. Things looked pretty grim for a second there."

"Eudora! Lucky!"

My eyes are drawn to the sky. A white blur flies past us and slams into the sand between us and Eudora. The impact kicks up a small sand cloud that covers our view of the duo. I try my best to see who had spoken, but the cloud makes it nearly impossible. A golden-hued green flash appears within the haze and I recognize it instantly. Somebody is using healing magic.

"Liaz!"

"I know!" Liaz gently shoves me behind himself and aims his pistol at the now dispersing sand cloud. "This is bad! Really bad!"

I look down as a spike-covered whip shoots up out of the ground beneath where we stand.

Liaz shoves me out of the way and I see the whip wrapped around him tightly. It locks his arms by his side and forces him to drop both of his pistols. Emerging from where the whip connects to the sand is a figure I don't recognize. They wear a dragon skull as a mask and a black jacket with a hood covering their head.

"It took you long enough, Sneaker." The cloud of sand settles back to the ground, revealing that both Eudora and Lucky are fully healed.

Standing away from me, helping Eudora back to her feet, is a figure that boils my blood. A jackal woman with grayish-bluish spotted fur, wearing a small leather jacket. It's the same woman from Wolfy's Tavern who sold us out: Spots.

"Woah!" Eudora is laughing hysterically, her face buried in one of her palms."You really tried to kill me! Hahahaha! You almost did it too!"

I prepare myself, my eyes flicking back and forth from Eudora and Spots to the man who has Liaz wrapped up. I can't tell what they are thinking. Eudora staggers back up to her normal posture, limping her arms. She has a wild expression on her face. Foam spews from her mouth corners. She's not laughing anymore.

"Now let's see you try that shit again!"

Chapter 39: Sixty Seconds

(Ironvine)

I look away for not even a second, seeing a blur slam down into the coliseum where Liaz and Whisperclaw are fighting. It doesn't matter. The simple curious look gives my opponent the opportunity to land a clean punch straight to my jaw. The sheer power behind the punch sends me sliding backwards. I spit out the blood I feel pooling in my mouth.

My opponent, a human man with an obviously unnatural muscular form, rushes me. Instead, when his foot hits the ground he stops moving. Suddenly, the air around him shakes violently and he sinks into the sand below. It's as if someone strapped a hundred ton vest onto his back.

"Need some help?" I see Goldenclaw, to my left, in my peripheral vision.

His paws glow with golden light and point at the man. I use the opportunity to look at the situation over at Whisperclaw and Liaz. It doesn't look well. Liaz is wrapped in a spike-covered whip. It doesn't seem to be cutting through his scales, but I notice that he has dropped both of his pistols.

Whisperclaw is standing ready, her claws out. In front of her, two women and a panther prepare to strike. They are clearly outmatched in a four vs two. It would probably be better if Goldenclaw helped them instead of me, I think. I look over at the man I've been fighting with until now. I can handle this guy alone.

"Actually, you should help Whisper and Liaz." I say, looking at Goldenclaw. "I got this."

"You sure?" He asks, concern written all over his face.

"Yeah, I'm sure." I smile. "Now go!"

Goldenclaw nods, letting his hands fall back to his sides, the glow slowly fading. I look back at the man as his fist collides with my jaw again. I try to retaliate by slicing upwards with my blade, but I'm still dazed by the punch. I completely miss and the man leaps away, out of range.

"I'm surprised you're still awake after that. Hahaha." The man laughs, his frizzy black and white afro swaying in the light wind. "That amount of power put your jackal friend to sleep last night."

Now that I'm watching the man flex his pale skinned, green vein covered muscles, this man looks like a creep. The thought of him putting a single finger on Whisperclaw sends waves of anger through my body. For the first time, I notice the blood-stained doctor's coat he's wearing.

"You're supposed to be a doctor, aren't you?" I ask, my gaze icy.

"Huh? What's this?" The man smiles widely. "Why does it matter? Oh! Don't tell me you actually want Doctor Fraken's special treatments?"

"I see." I say calmly. "So there's no point in reasoning with you then."

I see a vein bulge on Dr. Fraken's forehead. I don't really care if I upset him. The thought of this man being a doctor makes me want to snap him in half. I close my eyes, visualizing

Celestria's energy flowing through me and around me. I feel a tingling sensation running through my whole body and the pain in my face dissipates completely.

"Reasoning? Hahaha!" Dr. Fraken laughs loudly. "Why would I ever need to reason with someone so weak?"

"Celestria, I pray you'll forgive me for what I am about to do." I pray. "You told me to fight for what I deem right and right now, I know I have to stop this man to help my friends."

"Are you pitying me?" I barely hear Dr. Fraken in the background. "Do you know what I've done to achieve supreme power? I am the pinnacle of success! I am more knowledgeable than even the gods! How dare you look down on me?"

"Amen." I finish my prayer and slowly open my eyes.

"No! I look down on you! You are beneath me!" Dr. Fraken foams at the mouth.

His eyes roll back into his head. The bulging veins in his muscles grow significantly, as well as his muscles themselves. It looks like whatever he injected himself with is reacting to something else, probably his anger. It's causing his blood, filled with whatever mixture he created, to rush to his brain. He's losing his mind in real-time and probably has been losing his sanity slowly for only Celestria knows how long. I am confident that he will overdose within sixty seconds.

He rushes me, the ground ripping beneath his feet. He tries to grab me but his movements are sloppy. I sidestep and he misses me completely. I follow up with a quick elbow to his nose, which puts him on his back. Before he hits the ground, he performs a back flip. I try to jump back but his shoe tip clips my chin. For a moment, all I see are stars.

Through the stars, I somehow see his massive arm swinging towards me. I slip underneath and try to slash his stomach area. Dr. Fraken doesn't even see it coming. We separate, each heading in the opposite direction of the other. He is behind me now, our backs facing each other. I can hear him turn around, his arrogant voice transformed into mad snarling and screams. I don't turn to look at him, having already felt my blade carve through his gut. If the overdose doesn't kill him, he'll bleed to death instead. This fight is over.

"Arghhh!"

I hear Dr. Fraken cry out in agony and his feet shuffle. I instinctively dodge left, barely avoiding his beefy hands. As I counter with another slash, I see his face. He is like a raging beast, still attacking me even though his fate is sealed. If he had a little sanity left, he could retreat and heal himself, living to fight another day. I look into his rolled back eyes and see a single teardrop roll down his cheek. I am shocked, too stunned to move. This man, however sick, needs help.

"I'm sorry..." is the only phrase I can form.

The glimpse of humanity remaining in Dr. Fraken that I saw disappears instantly. I know it's too late to synthesize an antidote to whatever he injected himself with. However, I can ensure he doesn't suffer longer. My goal now has changed. I'm no longer stopping a mad doctor, instead I am helping a soul in need of salvation.

I throw my blade to the side. Dr. Fraken rushes me, burying his shoulder in my chest. I may not have fought for the past couple of years, but even I can see how telegraphed his movements are. I start to weave but decide against it, slamming my shoulder into his. Although he is massive for a human, us

Chim-Chi are known for our strength unparalleled by all but the giants. Our shoulders collide and Dr. Fraken drops to the floor, causing me to slide back a few feet. The overdose has reached its peak and he has little strength left to fight. I can tell by how his muscles and veins are deflating. His eyes are no longer rolled back and he seems back to being his usual self.

"Ugh!" He coughs up thick green fluid. "Dammit..."

"I wouldn't move too much." I say calmly, sitting down next to him. "You overdosed on whatever you injected yourself with."

"...Haha." He laughs dryly. "Tell Vanhiel...I'm sorry..."

"Sorry for what?" I ask, staring at him with a deep sinking feeling in my gut. "From what I can see, you fought for what you believed in. There's nothing wrong with that."

"Please..." Dr. Fraken coughs again violently. "...don't look at me with pity then."

I don't know what to say, so I look away. The coliseum is almost destroyed. The once full stands are now empty. Even still, different fights still take place. Whisperclaw, Goldenclaw, and Liaz fight their own opponents while the snargle man from before fights with Vanhiel. A fight that completely reshapes the terrain, even as we sit here in the charred sand.

"Do you think..." I look back at Dr. Fraken who reaches out towards the sky with a quivering hand. "...I'll see them again?"

"Hmm..." I ponder the question for a moment.

Before I can answer him, his arm falls limp next to his lifeless body. I sigh and stand up slowly, dusting the sand off my coat. Then I reach my hand out and close his still open eyes. At least now he can rest.

Chapter 40: How Much

(Glimmer)

"**D**o you know who this is?" Shane steps into the room behind me and closes the door. "This is Hawk Wind's son, named inheritor of the House of Wind. No bounty hunter in this city will bow to King Tomias without an order from him or his father. You would be wise to remember that."

"Why you insolent-"

"No, he's right." The knight with the striped feathers on his helm reaches for his sword, but the man with glasses grabs his arm. "We didn't come to start a war."

Thoughts race through my mind. I need to find a way to leave here. Everyone could need my help right now and I am trapped here with these people who want to turn me in for money.

"Like I told you boys earlier, all of the culprits of last night's rebellion were part of the Inner Circle." Shane says. "I don't care much for the king, none of us really do, but the Inner Circle ain't much better. Take last night for example. They rounded up everybody on the streets and took them to the dungeons."

"You were right to assume they were up to something." The man with the glasses releases the arm of his fellow knight. "I can think of a few reasons why someone would need a large group of people, and none of them are good."

"Okay, so you'll help, right?" Shane's face lights up with joy. "I know exactly where they're keeping everyone."

"Hold on." The man with the glasses grins a bit. "I never said we would help you... for free."

"I was right! You guys are just as corrupt as that Lord in Amacedia!" I shout. "You'll probably betray us as soon as we pay you!"

"I don't know what Lord you speak of, but me and my men are knights of the Sellsword guild that have no allegiance but to the laws of Ardent and to the ones who hire us." The man with the glasses quickly rises to his feet.

I jump back, expecting him to strike out, but he bows instead. All of the other knights look at him for a moment before doing the same.

"Please accept my apology on behalf of the Sellsword guild for any problems those in line with us may have caused. We may be hired hands, but we swear an oath to always uphold our agreements."

"How much?" Shane crosses his arms, disappointed.

"What?" The man raises his head.

"How much to help us free the people?" I repeat the question.

"It's a mighty undertaking, but we can make it happen for 1,000 gold coins." He responds. "Mighty generous I would say, since we're not getting a bounty for this one."

"1,000 gold? Are you crazy?" I'm fuming.

"We'll pay you 10,000 Gold Coins if you can help us take back control of the city and stop whatever the Inner Circle is up to." Shane cuts in. "But we'll only pay you after the job is done."

THE INNER CIRCLE

"Captain, I don't know."

"Silence Uriel." The man in the glasses looks sternly at the knight with the feathers. "We'll gladly accept your offer. We'll begin immediately if that is fine with you."

"Yes, of course. Thank you so much Mr. Loleo. I'm sure our prince would be more than happy to help you with any information you might need." Shane lightly nudges my shoulder. "Like I said before, I know exactly where the Inner Circle are keeping everybody. My sons saw them dragging some of the first ring women and children to the holding cells underneath the arena."

"Prince... Glimmer, wasn't it?" The man with the glasses turns towards me. "Do you know why they would take people under the arena?"

"Sorry, no." I shake my head, still a bit reluctant about giving away information to these people. "But I know that my friends and my dad are fighting Vanhiel and the others over there. My dad said something about..."

"...The Sovereign's Challenge. Yes, that makes sense." Shane pulls up a chair for me and himself. "Vanhiel can lawfully seize control of the House of Wind by defeating Hawk in the Sovereign's Challenge. Most bounty hunters who didn't side with the Inner Circle during the coup will likely side with them if Vanhiel kills Hawk."

"Hmm." Loleo narrows his eyes to me and strokes his chin. "That means our small political problem would be solved, wouldn't it? Isn't it possible for Vanhiel to just make the bounty hunters submit when he takes the throne?"

"No, he wouldn't." I say, clenching my fist to keep my anger inside. "Vanhiel doesn't even want to take the throne. He said he wanted all bounty hunters to decide their own fates. 'No more kings' were his exact words."

"So why put himself through all the trouble of competing in this Sovereign's Challenge?" Loleo stretches lazily. "It seems to me like he has already done what he set out to do. The only thing left is to kill the king and be done with it."

"Nobody would listen to him otherwise." Shane says matter of factly. "We would have searched for Prince Glimmer and crowned him king."

"Ha!" Loleo laughs. "You bounty hunters are so loyal to the House of Wind that it's scary."

I look at Shane, silent. I don't know much about Denzen, though I remember hearing stories about it as a child. Our home in the countryside was hundreds of miles from Vertalara, so me and Glam never saw it.

"Your precious King Hawk allegedly allowed human experimentation and illegally forced the kingdom's children to fight each other to death and you would still serve under his kin?" Loleo laughs so hard he starts crying.

"Our loyalty does not lay with King Hawk alone. As you have mentioned, he has allowed and even paid for unspeakable acts to be done to his own people." Shane places both hands on the table in front of him. "However, our loyalty lies with those in the House of Wind. That is why nobody has challenged Hawk yet. To those of us who call this city our home, the Wind Family members are revered as ancient Gods and their offspring are revered as the same. I will not bore you with the specifics, but that is why we serve King Hawk as we do."

"Alright, alright. I think I've got all the information I need." Loleo scratches his ear. "Way to kill the mood."

THE INNER CIRCLE

"So you will help us then?" Shane glances at me, smiling.

"Yes, we will help you." Loleo stands up, the knights around him following suit. "If I understand you both correctly, this Vanhiel guy will break the treaty if he takes over. That won't be helpful for business, so we'll save your king or make sure our young prince here takes his place."

"Thank you so much." Shane shakes Loleo's hand fervently, not letting go until Loleo rips it away. "Is there anything you guys need before you go?"

"Yes," Loleo grins at me with a mischievous look on his face. "We'll take the prince with us as a down payment. A map of the dungeon under the arena would be helpful too. We'll leave immediately after I get that from you."

"Wha-" Before I can argue, two of the knights closest to me grab me by the arms.

Chapter 41: See You Around

(Renald)

The senat jabs out with his longsword. I move my head slightly to the left, barely slipping by it and aiming for a slash with my own sword. I miss the slash but, mid-motion, I rotate into a side kick. My foot slams into the senat's side, causing his body to fold in on itself before he slides away. He holds his ground. The same faint blue aura that appeared around him last time slowly manifests.

"Where's all that ferocity you had a second ago?" He chuckles. "I know it's in you White knight. We all know. What happened, what you did that night."

I blink and the senat is right in front of me. I instinctively throw my shield up, but he's too fast. His longsword digs into my right shoulder. I feel a snap in my arm and am sent flying into the stands. I climb back to my feet, blood leaking down my arm. I position myself, gripping my sword with both hands. The senat is looking at me with a smile on his face, unmoving. He seems so sure of himself, of victory, but the bruise on his side tells another story. I lunge at him, stabbing him first. He parries my sword perfectly with his own and as I withdraw my blade to a defensive position, he comes down on my left collarbone. The blade sinks in deep and my whole body explodes with pain when he yanks it back out.

I try to stab him in the head, but I miss. It's as if he flashes out of reality for a split second. I feel his sword carve into my right side and I get flung from the stands back into the arena. My back crashes into the ground, pain shooting up and down my spine. I feel myself sliding across the sand, my body rolling over on top of itself until I slam into something. Now, looking down on me is Ironvine's emotionless face.

"Can you stand?" He asks me calmly, his body glowing in a similar faint aura as the senat's, but his is green instead of blue.

"I can try." I answer, strength flowing back into my body seemingly out of nowhere. "This doesn't make sense. I don't have nearly enough energy left to heal myself."

"It's Celestria. She has healed you this day." Ironvine helps me to my feet, his expression cold.

"No way!" My head snaps to the senat, who leaps down from the stands and approaches us. "You killed Fraken? I thought that old geezer would never die. Blackthorn'll be pissed when he hears this."

"Blackthorn?" I ask, surprised to hear that bastard's name again.

"Oh, oh, right. You guys don't know about that." The senat smirks. "Forget I even mentioned it."

"Ren." I feel Ironvine place his hand on my shoulder. "I'm about to give you some of Celestria's power."

I feel a sudden surge of energy fill my body, even more than when I woke up this morning. I smile at Ironvine and nod at him. I'm sure I can win now. I already feel my wounds closing.

"If you've got things handled here, I'm going to try to help beat that Vanhiel guy." Ironvine says, turning away from me and to the intense battle now unfolding in the sky above the coliseum.

"I wouldn't do that if I were you. He's stronger than all of you combined." The senat raises his eyebrows at Ironvine. "And after what we've got planned, he'll be able to absolutely destroy Hawk."

"If you say so." Is the only thing Ironvine says before he leaps onto the coliseum wall behind me and up into the air.

"Your friend is going to die, you know that right?" The senat smirks. "Oh, but you're pretty good at letting people die, aren't you?"

"You really talk too much." I say, allowing my rage to consume me one last time.

I know I have to end this guy quickly, before he can try to fight back. I feel my bloodlust skyrocket, my vision sharpens and everything fades to red. I feel my body lurch forward. I can barely percieve my own motions.

I can smell the senat's blood as my sword carves an X across his chest. I can feel the shift in the sand vibrations as he jumps back, but his blood is already in my hands. He swings his longsword at me, fear pouring out of his every motion. He doesn't even realize I'm behind him. I force his blood to form into two large, curved daggers which I slam into his back. I slide backwards and force the blood pouring out to form a giant javelin.

"Get-get away from me!" I can hear him scream.

I don't. I drive the javelin deep into his stomach and manage to kick him in the jaw. My vision is returning to normal. My heightened senses are fading rapidly. I can see the senat man clearly, with a massive, bloody X carved into his chest. He has two blood daggers sticking out of his back and a giant crimson javelin stuck in his stomach. The solidified blood weapons splash onto the ground, deforming. The senat is still standing however, despite all of his intense injuries.

"Blah-" Blood pours from his mouth. "-ha. Ha. That's more like it. That's the White knight I've heard so much about."

I can't move. My whole body feels numb. Dammit, I think, I overdid it. The senat dashes towards me and stabs me in the gut, grinning the whole time.

I stumble backwards, but every time I try to take a step the senat pushes his sword in a bit further. I try to swing my sword at him but I cannot lift my arm.

"A scar... " The senat finally pulls his sword out of my stomach and slashes me twice across the chest, forming an x. "... for a scar."

As the words leave his mouth, he collapses onto the ground. Blood puddles underneath him. I feel a burning sensation in my body. I can't stand the pain anymore and fall down next to him. This is it. I don't have enough energy to heal. My eyes search the coliseum, landing on Whisperclaw who fights against a senat woman and a large panther. My mind drifts back to the day I met her. The day I was sentenced to death. Her words echo in my mind like yesterday.

"Do you want to die? In that case, why don't you die for me?" She asked, reaching out her hand to me. "That way, we both have something to live for."

I can't die yet, not while she still needs help. I rise to my feet slowly, pain coursing through my body. I stumble over to the senat before collapsing again. I've never drunk blood before, but I'm about to try. I bite into the senat's flesh and drink. I drink until I am full.

After a while, I feel all of my strength returning. I also feel something else. Something I've never felt before. I relive memories that are not mine, memories of a young boy with gray skin. A senat with no horns. I recall flashes of the boy's life, first living on the streets, struggling to survive, then being taken in by a senat woman. Next, I see him as a young man fighting against others around his age. He killed them all. Then I see him being branded with a wind tattoo on his neck by Glimmer's father. When the visions stop, all I see around me is darkness. Through the darkness, I can see the senat man facing me, sitting cross-legged.

"Man you were strong." He laughs. "I got a few good hits though, right?"

"What's happening?" I ask, unsure of what to do.

"Isn't that obvious?" In frustration, he scratches his bald head. "Argh! This sucks... but at least I didn't get killed by someone weak."

I say nothing. How am I supposed to react here? I've never been skilled at dealing with stuff like this. I've never even been in this situation before.

"Hey..." The senat says, rising to his feet and turning away from me. "I don't think you'll beat him, but if you do, tell Vanhiel I said I'm sorry I wasn't strong enough and... if you ever meet her, tell the old lady not to worry too much."

I look down at the ground. I wish he could have died quietly like all the others. Why do I have to hear this?

"Hey!" I yell at him before he disappears into the distance.

"Hmm?" He turns around slightly.

"I think..." I don't even know why I'm saying this. "... I think you are really strong."

He looks back at me and smirks. Then he walks away, throwing a hand up as he disappears into the horizon.

"See you around kid. Don't die on me too fast."

Chapter 42: You Did This

(Whisperclaw)

"**I** was supposed to fight you, right?" Eudora's khopesh nearly slices my chest open. "Right? Why are you running now?"

I jump back to avoid her wild slash, but in the exchange I lose track of Lucky. That's until I feel his claws dig into my arm, carving a trio of deep cuts into my fur. I spin around, kicking out with both my feet and aiming at Lucky's nose.

Out of my peripheral vision, I see an orange light flash. I quickly slam my claws into the sand beneath me, stopping my momentum. This is right as Spots sends a massive fireball between me and Lucky. It continues for a moment before exploding into the coliseum wall. The wall erupts into flames that immediately spread to the stands, which are now completely empty.

"How are you still able to move?" My attention is drawn to Liaz, who is slowly standing up from the sand.

The figure with the dragon skull mask, named Sneaker I believe, takes a few steps back in fear. I guess something didn't work out as planned. From what I know, Liaz is a retired adventurer. I'm not a betting woman, but if I had to, I would bet that he is probably the strongest in our group at the moment. There's no telling what he's been through.

"Focus!" The blade of Eudora's khopesh shaves a bit of fur off my neck. "Otherwise, you might lose your head! Ha ha ha!"

I roll away from her and onto my feet. I can see Lucky getting ready to pounce in my peripheral vision. I prepare myself, but as he jumps onto me, the air around him shakes violently. I watch in shock as he is yanked down from the sky mid-jump and slammed into the sand below. The air around Lucky stops shaking, and in a blink I see Goldenclaw appear in front of me, knocking Eudora's khopesh away with his rapier. A golden aura seeps from the blade and, without saying a single word, Goldenclaw unleashes a fury of stabs and slashes on Eudora, Lucky, and Spots.

Eudora uses her newly healed wings to fly into the sky and out of Goldenclaw's reach. However, Spots and Lucky both take significant damage. Spots has a deep gash running diagonally up her face, across her nose. Lucky, on the other hand, gets stabbed in the back. Despite the serious injury, Lucky stands. It tries weakly to swipe at Goldenclaw, who calmly steps back and buries his rapier into Lucky's skull. Without a sound, Lucky falls to the ground. This time, he appears to be fully deceased.

I can see Eudora and Spots' pained expressions. I lunge at Spots, aiming to cut her eyes with my claws. She leans back, dodging my slash and pointing her index finger claw directly between my eyes.

"See you in hell, you bitch." She whispers and a red dot appears at the tip of her claw.

I lean all the way back, so far back that my feet touch my back. From Spots' claw, a long red beam fires. I can see it soar over me and shoot clean through the coliseum wall, like butter.

I flip into a back handspring, putting distance between us. I see Eudora charging towards Goldenclaw.

"I'll kill you!" She screams, tears streaming down her face as she stabs Goldenclaw multiple times. "Y-you killed my best friend, heartless fuck! I'll never forgive you for this!"

"If I recall correctly..." Goldenclaw nonchalantly dodges all attempted strikes. "... you tried to kill my friends first. That, my dear, is what killed your best friend. Your own foolish decision and the foolish decisions of those you align yourself with."

He parries Eudora's last strike and outstretches his palm. It glows with golden light and the air around Eudora quivers. She fights it for a second, flapping her wings as hard as she can. That second was just long enough for Goldenclaw to plunge his rapier into her chest.

"I hope it was worth it." He says softly, grabbing her by the waist and pulling her further onto the blade until it's sticking out of her back.

Then, he pulls his sword out and slices horizontally. Eudora's head slides off her neck, and her lifeless body crumples in the sand.

"No..." Spots steps away from us, but Goldenclaw appears behind her and attempts to stab her in the spine.

Before Goldenclaw can stab her, Ironvine's body slams into him. They both tumble across the sand, stopping just short of the flaming hole in the coliseum wall. I just barely dive out of Vanhiel's way, who crashes down seconds after Ironvine.

"Ye-yes!" I hear a mangled voice gasp. "Hiel! Help us!"

I look up from the spot on the ground I dived to. I see Liaz, with fresh cuts on his scales, holding up the dragon-masked figure by the throat. The figure is full of gunshot wounds and is bleeding heavily.

"They killed everyone!" Spots screams, running up to Vanhiel who struggles to stand. "Fraken, Ash, Eudora! They even killed Lucky!"

Another figure crashes from the sky in front of us, kicking up a small sandcloud around themselves. When the smoke clears, Glimmer's dad stands. He looks just as hurt as Vanhiel, both bruised and bloody.

"Is this what you wanted?" Glimmer's dad shouts the question, staring at Vanhiel. "You wanted everyone to die? You rebelled against me for... this? Don't you see how pathetic you look right now? Don't you see how much pain and death you've caused?"

"Like you're better than me!" Vanhiel roars. "You took everything from us! You made Fraken lose his mind because he didn't want to experiment on our people, so you forced him to experiment on himself! You turned Eudora into a whore! Then you made Ash and Spots fight for their lives as children! You did this!"

Liaz tosses Sneaker at Vanhiel's feet and helps me stand up. I can see Goldenclaw and Ironvine standing back up as well. Behind Glimmer's dad, I can see Renald, now shirtless, lying motionless in front of the gray skinned senat's mutilated body. Unlike the senat, Renald has no open wounds.

"I..." Glimmer's dad hesitates. "...I'm sorry."

"Really? Hahahaha!" Vanhiel laughs hysterically. "You're sorry? No, no, no, no, no. You'll be sorry! You don't even know half of it! The deal I had to take to get this far! Oh hoho, but you will! Everyone will!"

THE INNER CIRCLE

As if cued by Vanhiel's speech, the ground shakes all around us. I look over at Goldenclaw, but his hands aren't glowing. I don't know what's happening but something doesn't feel right.

"Everyone run!" Goldenclaw yells. "The sand is sinking!"

"Sorry, but nobody is moving anywhere." Chills shoot down my spine, the sound of a familiar, bored voice echoing from the stands at the front of the coliseum.

I look up to see where the voice is coming from and spot Blackthorn, sitting with his legs crossed in the stands. He has on a white, button up collared shirt and black pants. In one hand, he holds a small plate and in the other is a cup with a hot substance inside that he drinks from. He places the cup on the plate and sticks his hand out towards us.

"Vanhiel…" He calls out. "… I believe this settles our debts. I will take my scroll back as soon as you get out of sight. I assume you will do what needs to be done after that, so I will do the same."

His paw glows purple and I feel a crushing weight suddenly appear on top of me. I fall down to my knees, all my attention devoted to keeping upright. Goldenclaw was right. I can sense the sand loosening up and my body sinking into it. I use all of my strength to look up again, finding Renald. Then I feel the sand slip out from underneath me completely and I barrel down, towards the newly formed pit at the bottom of the coliseum.

Chapter 43: This Ends Now

(Ironvine)

The last thing I remember was Vanhiel and Hawk arguing. I remember Blackthorn appearing in the stands. Then I felt a crushing weight unlike anything I'd experienced before, pinning me to the sand. With no way to escape, the sand suddenly collapsed beneath my feet and I felt myself falling. Then everything fell dark. I slowly open my eyes. Every part of my body aches.

I am in a circular room, the same size as the coliseum we were in earlier. I spot Renald's unconscious body, buried beneath a pile of golden sand. Whisperclaw, who looks alright, is digging him out. Goldenclaw, who was standing next to me when the floor collapsed, is standing back up. I see Liaz across the room doing the same. I don't find Vanhiel, the jackal woman he was with, the figure in the dragon skull mask, or Hawk. Looking up, I can see the sun beaming down on us through the massive hole we fell through.

"Where in Abell's name are we?" Liaz asks, dusting himself off and picking up his pistols.

"Underneath the arena, I assume." Goldenclaw answers, shaking the sand out of his mane. "Is everyone alright?"

"Ironvine! Renald-" Whisperclaw calls out panicked. "He... he's not waking up!"

I rush over to where she cradles Renald's head in her lap. He is shirtless now and a massive X scar is carved into his chest. I extend my hands and imagine Celestria's energy covering him. I let it sit over him for a few moments, but he doesn't budge. I feel his pulse. His heartbeat is steady and he's breathing well. I can't find a single reason why he isn't waking up.

"I don't know." I say, completely unsure of my diagnosis for the first time since becoming a doctor. "He seems fine. I don't know why he isn't waking up though."

"If he's alive, we can escape, right?" Goldenclaw says. "We brought some teleportation feathers from the dungeon. We should be able to teleport to Glimmer and I can get us to Ulric. It's the closest city to the boss room."

"No." Whisperclaw answers. "We promised Glimmer we'd save his dad. We're not leaving until we know he's safe."

"That's easier said than done. We don't even know where they went." Goldenclaw argues. "If I'm being honest, Hawk doesn't seem like the most brilliant king either. Should we really help him?"

"I think these guys are rubbing off on you Gold." Liaz laughs. "Back in the day, you never questioned a King."

"We're not doing it for him." Whisperclaw snaps. "We're doing it for Glimmer. I could care less about what happens in this city."

"She's right," I say. "Glimmer is our teammate, so if we can help him, we should."

"You make it sound so simple." Liaz laughs. "Whelp, let's get to it shall we? There's only one way they could have gone."

Liaz points at the entrance to a long hallway built into the back wall of the room. I step back from Renald's body and give Whisperclaw space to stand up. She looks at Renald and frowns.

"He'll be ok." I assure her. "He's safer here than coming with us. There's no telling what we're about to walk into."

"Y-yeah." She nods.

We leave the room and enter the hallway. At the end, it veers to the right, leading us to a set of stairs going further down. We move stealthily, following the only path available to us. The stairs lead to another large circular chamber. As we approach, I hear a gunshot followed by a flash of blue light through the open doorway.

"Vanhiel, I don't know what you're scheming but this ends now!" I hear Hawks' voice echoing down the hall.

Me and Whisperclaw look at each other before sprinting into the room. Hawk is standing a few steps ahead of us, facing Vanhiel who is floating in the middle of the air. He is holding the body of the figure in the dragon skull mask in one hand. In his other hand is a mana pistol with smoke streaming from the end. He points at the body of the Jackal woman who was with him before the coliseum floor collapsed. She has tears streaming down her face and a massive gunshot wound in her chest. I can tell by her eyes that she's dead.

"You're so right! It ends now!" Vanhiel screams. "I sacrificed everything for this one moment! This single chance!"

Suddenly, the wall behind Vanhiel rises. On the other side is a square-shaped room filled with hundreds, if not thousands of women and children. They are all incapacitated, lying unconscious on the ground. Each of them has a chain connected to one of their legs or arms. Each chain is connected to a single peg attached to the ceiling. Drawn around the peg is an intricate circle made of blood with a language written around it that I do not immediately recognize. In each corner of the room is a large obsidian pillar with a point at the end.

"Have you lost your mind?" Hawk screams. "You dare imprison our people? Innocent women and children?"

"I didn't want it to come to this." Vanhiel says with a hint of sadness in his voice. "You couldn't die with honor. You had to be the supreme Hawk Wind of the House of Wind until the end. Well, now look! This is every single woman and child who can use magic in Denzen! And you will watch them sacrifice themselves to turn me into a God!"

Vanhiel throws the body of the figure he's holding in his hand down next to the jackal woman. Then, in a flash of blue light, he shoots the figure in the head.

"No!" Goldenclaw yells. "You would kill your own teammate? I thought they were your friends!"

Blood spills from the figure's body. Suddenly the ground around them glows with an eerie black light. The light rapidly engulfs them both and then shoots up into the sky around Vanhiel.

"This is some kind of ritual!" Hawk turns to us. "Whatever it takes, we have to stop him from completing it!"

"Already on it." Liaz dashes forward and unloads bullets into the black light, but they disintegrate immediately.

I run around it and into the room with all the women and children. Right when I'm about to cross the entrance, I feel a numbing sensation spread over my entire body. I am sent flying backwards, away from the room. Black sparks crackle around the entryway. The same black light around Vanhiel is now being pulled from the women and children through the chains. I can see it flowing from the ceiling into the four pillars and back into the ground. I assume the pillars power the ritual.

"Guys, we have to destroy those pillars!" I call out from behind me. "I can't enter the room. There's some kind of force-field keeping me out."

"I don't think we have time for that." I turn at Whisper-claw's statement.

The black light around Vanhiel is changing, shrinking. It disconnects from the ground completely and forms into a ball, suspended in the air. I feel a shiver run down my spine. This definitely isn't okay. Sparks of blue energy crack around the ball as it gets smaller. In a matter of seconds, the ball has completely transformed into a humanoid creature. Then the black light bursts like a bubble. Now hovering over us is unlike anything I've ever seen before. It's a figure reminiscent of Vanhiel, but instead of yellow scales, it has smooth metallic silver skin. Embedded on their chest, abs, and torso are three shiny black orbs. They have no mouth and no clothes, but also no distinguishable parts. The figures' hands look like gauntlets with jagged claws. Their eyes are pitch black and they have a long beard full of silver hair. On its back are two silver wings, like dragon wings, and connected to its head are two large silver horns.

"Va-Vanhiel?" Hawk asks, obviously unsure about the situation.

"Hawk Wind of the House of Wind." Vanhiel disappears from the sky and appears directly in front of Hawk, looking deep into his eyes, his mouth unmoving. "Are you afraid of death?"

Chapter 44: Surprise

(Glimmer)

"Keep it moving kid." One of Loleo's knights shoves me. "We don't have all day. Hurry up, before we're all captured for Abell's sake."

I am too focused on the smoke barrelling out of the coliseum to care. We snuck into the fourth ring successfully. It's me, Loleo, and 11 of his knights. The knight with feathers on his helm, Uriel, was left behind with Shane and the others. Loleo thought it would be better to travel with less people, to avoid detection. The look on his face right now says otherwise.

"Please, Loleo -" I say, reaching for his shoulder.

"Don't move!" One of the knights cuts me off, drawing his sword in the same motion he uses to step in between Loleo and myself.

"Please sir, let me get my flute from the dungeon before we go further." I plead. "My friends are in the coliseum right now helping my dad. If I can get our weapons and my flute, we can help you. Without my flute, I-"

"That's enough." Loleo says without turning around. "The answer is no. We will not discuss this further. Now move it."

Everyone runs towards the entrance to the coliseum, dipping and dodging through the different vendor stalls throughout the street. I follow, but I try to lag behind a bit. I have to get our supplies if I'm planning to help. Right now, I just need a good escape plan.

"Genamax, chain the kid." I hear one of the knights behind me.

Before I can make a break for it, a bulky knight almost triple my size slams a massive chain together around me. I hear it lock into place and my body jerks. I fall onto the ground, hitting my shoulder on the cobblestone.

"Get up. We will all get caught if you don't move." I look up at Loleo, who stares down at me. "We're almost there."

I feel my body lifted off the ground. I rotate myself and see the bulky knight, Genamax, hosting me on his shoulder. I feel sick. Every step he takes, his shoulder plate pushes the chain into my stomach. After a few more minutes of non-stop running, Genamax finally puts me down in front of a massive crater where the coliseum interior used to be.

"No..." I say, falling to my knees. "... Everyone was here. My dad, Renald, Whisperclaw, Ironvine, everyone."

"Don't freak out yet." I look at Loleo, who touches my shoulder. "Look at the way the ground disappeared. It all fell perfectly along the fighting area. None of the stands, where bystanders would be, fell with it. It probably leads underground."

"Sir, then..." The knight who drew his sword on me whispers. "... do you think it's true? What Shane said?"

"It's possible." Loleo looks at me, then at Genamax. "Release the prince, Gena."

"But sir-" Genamax protests but is silenced by Loleo's firm look.

"I'm splitting us into two teams from here," he says. "Gena, Dawn, Asteroid, and Issiah, you will travel with the prince to retrieve his and his friend's belongings. The rest of us will travel below. We leave immediately."

"Yes sir." The knights say.

Genamax undoes my chains and helps me stand up. The other 3 knights form a small circle around us.

"Where to, oh mighty prince?" They laugh.

I brush myself off and walk towards Loleo. I don't even know where I'm heading, but Shane gave him a map.

"Hey, can I look at the map?" I ask.

"Hmm?" Loleo looks over his shoulder at me. "Sure kid. I don't need it anymore anyway."

He tosses the map, a large scroll glued to two wood planks, over his shoulder. It lands on the ground in front of me, and I scramble to pick it up. It does nothing to stop the knights' giggles. I walk back over to Genamax and the others, unrolling the map. I probably spend about 10 minutes trying to understand it, which I don't.

"Gods, kid. Can't you do anything useful?" One of the knights, who holds a spear instead of a sword, complains. "Give it here."

They snatch the map out of my hands and look at it. They turn to some of the others, pointing out a few details in silence. A few nods, a few hand motions towards the map. Eventually, they hand the map back to me.

"Alright guys, we're headed below." They say, motioning everyone close. "We'll use the sewers as an entry point. Let's move."

Everyone turns and sprints out of the coliseum, towards a nearby sewer drain. I follow along, trying to match their brisk pace, but failing miserably. Genamax pops the lid off the drain and, one after another, the knights jump in. I climb down second to last, with Genamax behind me. My feet splash into waist high water, about knee height for the knights. Everyone has to crouch down except me.

"Issiah, light." The knight who has led us says.

"On it." The knight named Issiah sheaths their sword.

They extend their left hand out in front of them. Issiah slowly rotates his hand around. I can see sparks beginning to fly from his gauntlet. Then suddenly, his hand burst into flames. The entire sewer is illuminated in a bright orange glow.

"Alright everyone, let's move. This should be an in and out mission." The leader says, leading us through the narrow sewer passage.

We continue for a few minutes. Nobody says a word, we all just follow the person in front of us. Soon we reach a set of bars, preventing us from continuing further. Without saying anything, the knight at the front slices a square into the bars. They clatter to the floor with no resistance at all. We all squeeze through, with the rest pulling Genamax.

"Alright, we should reach the main intersection of the dungeon." The leader whispers. "This should also connect us to the catacombs below. We'll meet Captain Loleo there."

We all nod. I'm anxious. More than I've ever been before. What is happening with everyone? I keep walking, following the knights. We reach a large opening where sewer water drops below. An orange light shines through the opening, illuminating familiar stone passageways below. The leader motions at Issiah, who quickly extinguishes the flames on their hand. We each drop down into the passageway below. The leader jumps down first and everyone but Genamax comes down after. When I jump down, one of them catches me before I hit the ground, helping me land softly on my feet.

We keep moving, following the passageway to our left. It winds around, leading us past a hallway lined with cells. The same types of cells that me, Whisperclaw, Renald, and my dad were in mere hours ago. We reach a large set of double doors at the end of the hallway. The leader nods at Genamax, who pushes past us and rams his shoulder into it. The doors creak loudly under his weight, cracking and splitting but not breaking. Genamax steps back and rams his shoulder into the doors again. This time, they fly off the hinges and skid across the stone floors. This reveals a large chamber full of items stacked in different piles.

"Make it fast, kid." The leader says to me, pointing into the room. "Find your things and let's get out of here."

"Dawn, something doesn't feel right." I hear Issiah whisper to the leader, who must be Dawn. "Where are all the guards?"

We all freeze as clapping fills the room, getting closer. Walking around one of the piles is a saber with black fur, a scar across his closed right eye, clapping his paws together slowly. I recognize his face immediately, from the night we escaped from Amacedia. It's Blackthorn. The air around us suddenly vibrates and I feel a crushing weight slam onto my back. All of us are pinned to the floor, except for Genamax who visibly shakes as he struggles to stand.

"This is a surprise." Blackthorn chuckles. "It's the snargle who stole from me."

He steps over us. As he does, I see the ethereal enchantment scroll tucked into the collar of his white button-up shirt. I scream in anger, as it's the only thing I can do. The pressure on my chest keeps me from moving, talking, or breathing properly.

"I would love to play with you all, but we'll call it even." Blackthorn laughs, his voice drifting away from us. "Your friends are all about to die after all."

The pressure disappears. I leap to my feet and spin around, searching for that slime, but I don't see him anywhere. He slipped away from us again.

Chapter 45: My Stupid Mistake

(Renald)

My eyes snap open. I can smell the blood of 8 figures descending on top of me. I am in a large, empty, circular pit. All around is sand and bones, just like inside the coliseum. I see Ash's body a few feet away. He is partially covered in sand, like some fell on him. I see the unmoving human body with white hair further away, also covered in sand. I look around quickly, searching for any signs of Whisperclaw or the others, but all I can find are the bodies of the red and white skinned senat woman, who fought Whisperclaw, her panther, and the giant skeleton of a rampaging undead dragon.

The figures are getting closer, moving faster than before. I breathe deeply, searching the air for familiar scents. It's faint, but I still pick it up. Whisperclaw and Ironvine, plus they seem to be in the same location. I glance at the figures, wondering whether or not it would be smart for me to kill them before they cause any trouble for us. Three large ropes plop down into the room, stopping just above the floor. I choose to let them live, following the smell of Whisperclaw's blood into a hallway built into the back wall of the room.

I follow the hallway, veering right and eventually heading down stairs. My foot touches down on the first step and I begin to hear the sounds of a fight below. I can feel an unnatural amount of mana surging from beneath the ground like a wind gust, sending chills down my spine. It reminds me of a time when I felt a similar burst of mana as a child. A wave of fear crashes over me. It can't be, I think, breaking out into a sprint down the stairs. I turn the corner and slide to a stop, just in time to catch Whisperclaw as she crashes down into my arms.

In the middle of the room is a figure with smooth metallic silver skin. Embedded on their chest, abs, and torso are three shiny black orbs that I recognize instantly. As I expected, it's the same as back then. I can smell the blood within the figure and I already know who they used to be. However, that isn't Vanhiel anymore. It's something much different.

The situation is obvious enough for me to figure out what to do. Vanhiel, or what used to be Vanhiel, holds Glimmer's dad up by the throat. Ironvine, Liaz, and Goldenclaw are currently circling him, unable to attack without putting Hawk at risk.

"Renald…" I look down at Whisperclaw, who is still in my arms. "…What happened to your eyes?"

"Huh?" I ask, unsure of what to make of her question. "Nevermind. I need you to do me a favor."

"Sure, what is it?" She asks, turning back around to face Vanhiel.

"I want you to take the others and run." I say, trying to stay calm. "I don't have time to explain, but you guys can't stay here."

"Nobody is leaving, son of House Black." Vanhiel's head suddenly turns towards me. "If I allowed you to leave here now, there would be no one to witness my ascension."

My body moves independently, faster than I could have imagined. In a fraction of a second, I shift from standing next to Whisperclaw to feeling the heel of my foot slam into the Ascent Core on Vanhiel's chest. There's a loud crack and a gust of wind explodes from the crystal and sends me flying backwards. Vanhiel roars in pain, throwing Glimmer's father away like a doll. I land on my feet, next to Whisperclaw.

"I said run!" I yell, putting as much force as I can muster into my voice. "Now! Before he recovers!"

Instead of running, I see Goldenclaw step up and unleash a flurry of attacks against Vanhiel. Cutting and stabbing all over his body with his rapier. It does nothing, however. All of his strikes bounce off Vanhiel's silver skin.

"None of my attacks can pierce his skin!" Goldenclaw calls out, still slashing and stabbing away.

"Switch with me." Liaz and Goldenclaw trade places in one of Goldenclaw's strikes. "This is where we should aim."

Liaz fires two shots from his pistols. The first shot bounces off the second and they both bounce around the room. It looks good. Both bullets move towards Vanhiel. Wait a second, I think. Vanhiel's not in the same spot anymore. I never saw him move. The mana bullets hit the spot where Vanhiel should have been and fizzle out, quickly followed by a horrified scream.

Vanhiel used the split second Goldenclaw backed off to get close to Liaz. My vision turns red when I see his claws sticking through Liaz's chest. I scream. Everything seems to move blurry around me. I launch myself at Vanhiel as quickly as I can. For a second, I can see him moving away and I instantly punch the crystal orb on his stomach before he can dodge.

"Take that, you-" An explosion of energy throws both me, Goldenclaw, and Liaz's limp body backwards.

I land hard on my back and slide into Whisperclaw who tries to help me up. As I stand, I see Glimmer's dad reach out his hand and slice across the air.

"Vanhiel!" He yells. "This is between you and me! Leave everyone else out of it! Let the women and children leave, and I might let you live!"

Exactly where Glimmer's dad sliced through the air, a large tear of darkness rips open and a massive skeleton steps out. In its hands is a large scythe made of bones. It has multiple layers of black cloth covering its entire body, except for its arms and face.

"Kill! Kill!" The skeleton says in a low, ominous tone. "Kill!"

Vanhiel looks back at the skeleton over his shoulder, as the skeleton jams the tip of its scythe into Vanhiel's third orb. He screams in pain, clawing at his own face. Another energy explosion bursts from Vanhiel, turning the skeleton into dust on contact. Me and Whisperclaw hold our ground against the wind gusts kicked up by the explosion, but just barely.

"We've got you now!" Goldenclaw yells. "You're not going anywhere!"

I see him across from us, on the other side of the room. Vanhiel has a small crater around himself due to earlier explosions. Goldenclaw points his paws at Vanhiel, both covered in golden light. The air around Vanhiel quivers and the crater sinks lower and lower into the ground, but Vanhiel looks completely unfazed.

"Ren, hold on tight." Whisperclaw says as she pulls me backwards. "We're about to kill that bastard, right now."

Instead of hitting the ground, everything turns dark around me. Then I'm falling through the sky, directly on top of Vanhiel. I expand my wings, stopping my fall. Below me, I see Whisperclaw land on Vanhiel. He adjusts slightly, avoiding her claws. I can also see Ironvine running over to Liaz's motionless body. He gets to where the body is and punches it with a fist covered in a green aura. The hole in Liaz's chest closes and he jerks upright and coughs blood.

"You will all bow to me." Vanhiel's metallic voice echoes around in my brain. "Resistance is futile."

Vanhiel's wings jerk unnaturally and the scales suddenly stand upright, like a porcupine's quills. Suddenly, a cluster of scales hit me in rapid succession, starting in my stomach and ending in my right shoulder. A pain unlike anything I've ever felt shoots through my entire body. My wings fall limp and I crash into the ground. My body shakes uncontrollably. My bones feel like they are burning. I can't move. I can't think. My vision is blurry. Everything hurts, but I try to stand up anyway.

Slowly, I manage to remove each of the silver coated scales one by one. I can see everything happening around me in slow motion. With every scale I remove, my vision clears slightly and the pain lifts. I notice Liaz shooting with his pistol from his position on the ground. Five, six, seven, eight. I see Whisperclaw reaching out to me, a scale in her left arm and paw.

I pull the last scale out of my chest and my senses return to normal simultaneously. I hear Liaz's gunshot followed by Whisperclaw screaming my name. I look down at myself, and for the first time ever, my wounds aren't closing. My hands tremble. A feeling of helplessness creeps into my gut. No matter what I do, I can't move. My body won't listen to me. I realize now that I made a mistake, dragging everyone into this impossible situation. My stupid mistake is the reason we're all about to die.

Chapter 46: After Today

(Whisperclaw)

I'm reaching out to Renald. He's screaming so much—much more than I've ever heard. Now that I think about it, I've never heard Renald scream in pain before now. It's horrifying. Renald convulses violently on the ground, his body twisting in an agonizing, nightmarish dance. The sound of his screams pierces through the air, more visceral and horrifying than anything I've ever experienced. His blood seeps into the earth, staining the ground red. Unlike the swift healing we witnessed in the colosseum, his wounds remain open and festering. When Vanhiel shot his scales out of his wings, a burst of air flung us away from him and away from each other. The only ones I see still standing are Ironvine and Glimmer's Dad.

"I call upon you in my time of need!" Glimmer's dad shouts, holding his hand straight up into the air with his palm open. "Join me and lend me your power to smite my enemies and those who rise up against me!"

"Took you long enough." A deep, dark voice, I've never heard before, booms over the entire room.

A deep, resonant voice echoes through the room, commanding immediate attention. A blinding streak of purple light pierces the ceiling, sending debris cascading to the ground. As the smoke clears, a tall, skeletal figure emerges, draped in a sharp black suit and a striking violet tie. The skeleton leans on a golden cane with a black, curved handle and a striking purple metal band. Its hollow eye sockets are filled with swirling darkness, and its razor-sharp teeth glisten with a sinister polish.

"That's right everybody, give it up. Give it up. No need to stand." The skeleton says in the same deep voice as earlier. "Death has arrived."

"Avarice..." I stare at Vanhiel, who dodged Liaz's mana bullet. "Do not interfere. This matter has nothing to do with the gods of old."

"Oh, is that so?" The skeleton skips over to Glimmer's dad and drapes his arm over his shoulder, bending down to do so. "Abell would be pissed if he heard that one. Yup."

"I'm warning you."

"Shut up, woulda?" The skeleton jabs his pinky into the empty socket where his left ear should be and twists it. "I don't think you get it. Got it? If I leave now, after hearing what you just said, Abell would toss me into the abyss for eternity. Plus, I've got a contract to uphold."

I'm too stunned to speak, as is everyone else apparently. Did he just call himself... Death? I ask myself over and over throughout the conversation. Before I can wrap my head around what's happening, the skeleton becomes semi-transparent and merges with Glimmer's dad. At first, a subtle tremor ripples through Glimmer's dad's body, but it quickly intensifies. His skin tightens over his bones, pulling taut until it almost seems translucent. Dark, twisted horns pierce through his scalp with a sickening crack, curling upward as his entire frame stretches unnaturally. He towers over everyone now, his spine elongating with each vertebra clicking into place, muscles and bones shifting grotesquely. His eyes sink deep into their sockets, voids of endless darkness. His fingers stretch out, the skin peeling away to reveal jagged, skeletal claws that gleam wickedly in the dim light. Then his mouth fuses, his lips melting into his face. This leaves behind a terrifying maw of gleaming gold, where razor-sharp fangs interlock like predator jaws. The skeleton's staff appears in mid-air, and Glimmer's dad catches it and points it at Vanhiel.

"18 seconds, betrayer." His voice echoes from within his body, a mix of Glimmer's dad's and the skeleton's. "18 seconds until retribution."

The ground trembles violently as bones erupt from the earth, latching onto Glimmer's dad and forming a grotesque exoskeleton. Then he steps forward slowly, disappears from my vision, then reappears in front of Vanhiel. In the same motion, he hits Vanhiel in the jaw with his cane handle, sending him flying back.

"You dare attack me?" Vanhiel screams the question, slamming his claws into the ground and using his wings to stop his momentum.

He glares at Renald, who has finally managed to get up. Vanhiel's eyes flash with a fleeting silver glow, his face twisting into panic. The once-solid silver armor encasing him ripples and peels away, revealing the yellow scales beneath in a disturbing display of vulnerability. I look back at Renald and see his eyes flash with the same silver as Vanhiel's right before all emotion evaporates from his face.

"Everyone, don't let this chance escape!" I hear Goldenclaw yell, but all I can focus on is Renald.

Something isn't sitting right with me. He's changed; I can smell it. I run over to him, dodging Ironvine, who rushes past me towards Vanhiel. I grab Renald by the shoulder and shake him back and forth. He doesn't respond. His eyes are completely without expression.

"Renald!" I yell, trying to snap him out of whatever trance he's in. "Ren! Come on, you can't do this to me right now! We need you!"

He doesn't even look at me. Instead, he stares into the distance. My heart is pounding in my chest. Renald's vacant gaze and emotional detachment echo a haunting, gut-wrenching loss. The fear of losing him, just as I lost Brownblood, engulfs me.

"Whisperclaw, focus!" Ironvine's voice pierces through my daze, pulling me back to the present.

Ironvine swings at Vanhiel, but Vanhiel dodges nimbly.

He slides behind Ironvine on his knees, spins, and slashes across Ironvine's back with his claws. I see blood pouring out of the gaping wound. It's so deep that I can see pieces of Ironvine's spine poking through. He stumbles forward and falls over, onto his side.

"Whisperclaw, help Ironvine!" Liaz shouts, stumbling to his feet. "I'll cover you!"

He fires a barrage of bullets at Vanhiel. I look back at Renald again before shadowstepping to Ironvine. His blood is staining his purple fur a dark red. He gazes up at me with fading strength, his eyes barely open.

"My...bag." He gasps, blood dripping from his mouth.

"Just stay awake for me." I plead, flipping him onto his back and digging into his pouch for healing pills.

As I fumble through Ironvine's pouch, I feel a sudden shift in the air. My instincts scream at me, but it's too late. A sickening, wet sound fills the space between heartbeats—metal sinking into flesh. My body freezes as I slowly turn, my breath catching in my throat. Standing above Ironvine's writhing form is Renald. A crimson saber juts from Ironvine's stomach, the blade slick with blood, still quivering from the strike. Renald holds the weapon with unsettling ease, his face without emotion. His golden eyes, once familiar, now gleam with cold detachment. I search his expression for any sign of remorse, recognition-anything. But there's nothing. Just mechanical precision as he yanks the blade free. The sound of flesh tearing is almost drowned out by my heart beat.

"No!" I scream, tears of anger and confusion streaming down my face. "Why?! Why would you do that?"

Renald glares at me silently, his golden eyes clearly dilated with silver flakes floating around. He turns the blade edge towards me. I don't have time to react as he attempts a slash, but thankfully I don't have to. Glimmer's dad appears in front of me and blocks it mid-swing by catching it with his index finger and thumb.

"You didn't strike me as weak-willed, vampire." Glimmer's dad says to Renald.

Renald's face shifts from emotionless to angry instantly. He screams, allowing his rage to shine through. I can see that he has large and sharp fangs on full display while screaming. I feel a mix of shock, dread, and regret settle in my stomach. Glimmer's dad called Renald a vampire, but I didn't know vampires had horns and wings. If Renald is a vampire, why have I never seen him drink blood before? Glimmer's dad smacks Renald's blood saber out of the way and chops him in the neck with a single motion. I can see his eyes roll back, then he falls to the ground limp. Glimmer's dad looks over at Vanhiel, an expression of hatred engraved on his face.

"That was a cheap trick." He says.

Glimmer's dad steps forward blindingly, reappearing directly in front of Vanhiel. He aims the tip of his cane at Vanhiel's head. Fear flashes in Vanhiel's eyes just before the cane's end erupts in a shroud of suffocating darkness, consuming him in an explosion of shadow. I desperately fumble through Ironvine's pouch, my hands shaking as I retrieve the healing pills. With frantic urgency, I force them into his mouth. Slowly, the bleeding stops, and his breathing stabilizes. Relief washes over me as I see the wounds close. As I glance back at Renald, now lying motionless amidst the chaos, a chilling sense of finality settles over me. The calmness of his repose contrasts starkly with the turmoil surrounding us. It's clear that today marks the beginning of a new, unpredictable chapter for us all.

Chapter 47: Hello Reality

(Ironvine)

I feel cold, endless, and empty. A brief memory flashes through my mind. I see Whisperclaw looking down at me, her hands moving frantically. Behind her, I can discern the blurry outline of a shadowy figure with glowing yellow eyes. The figure raises a sword, preparing to strike down. I shove Whisperclaw out of the way and feel the blade plunge into my gut. I cough, blood flying out of my mouth and onto the face of my attacker. They are no longer blurry. Instead, I see Renald standing over me.

I try to speak, but words elude me. Then, before I know it, I feel myself pulled backwards. Renald fades away into the distance and darkness envelopes my vision again. I keep falling on and on until I feel my body slow. I look down and see a bright white light. My feet touch the light, and I can stand. It's as if the light itself is solid beneath me. The light spreads all around me, blinding me. I squeeze my eyes shut and shield my face with my hands. It doesn't help. The light grows brighter and brighter. It reaches the point where I can no longer stand. I drop to my hands and knees, sweat pooling around my fur. I can only think that this is what death feels like. As the light slowly dissipates into a single source in front of me. I open my eyes. I am inside a massive, cavern-like structure. On either side of the structure are two pillars. Wrapped around the cavern is a massive woman I would recognize anywhere.

"You have returned to me again, my chosen champion." Celestria says weakly.

Her skin is paler than last time I saw her. The green in her veins seems to pulse, like a heart. Her light is dimming as well. That much is painfully obvious to me.

"Once more, I found my way to you accidentally." I smile.

"I would laugh, I promise." Celestria lets out a deep, hollowed breath, her eyes drifting close before opening again. "However, as you can see, I'm not in the most ideal condition at the present moment."

"Am I dead now?" I ask, looking at the gaping hole in my stomach. "I mean, Renald killed me. Didn't he?"

"He did try," she says. "Then again, he didn't. Not in his mind anyway."

"So I'm not dead?" I wipe my face. "Where am I then?"

"We are deep beneath the ground." Celestria looks away from me, gazing into the distance. "It was once a sacred place, a place for me to replenish the tower's mana wellsprings. Now, it is the place I will die."

I look at the ground. I already saw this coming, I just didn't want to say anything. I never do. Gazer said it was a personal weakness as a doctor. I can't bear to look at a patient's face if I have to give a negative diagnosis.

"You don't look surprised." Celestria chuckles dryly. "You're smart, so I assumed you already had a hunch."

"I did, but I had hoped you could be healed if possible." I say, unable to keep my sadness from leaking into my voice.

"You're a goddess aren't you? Can't you heal yourself or something?"

"There are some weapons in this world that are powerful enough to slay a goddess like myself." She answers calmly. "This tower is full of more danger than you could possibly imagine."

"Like Vanhiel." I murmur. "That thing is a monster."

"He has been corrupted by ancient dark magic." Celestria says, with a bit of urgency in her tone. "His link to the ritual was severed, but he is still dangerous."

"What should I do?" I ask. "He's so strong. I feel like I can't fight him, even with your power."

"Then you must get stronger, my champion." She looks at me and I can see sadness in her eyes. "In a few months, me and my powers will likely be a memory. That means you must learn to rely on yourself, for I cannot save you."

I feel something tug my body upwards, just slightly. Celestria smiles at me and winks her eyes.

"The time has come for you to return to the land of the living," she says. "Be courageous, my chosen champion. Victory is more achievable than you think."

"Thank-" My body gets yanked into the sky, through the cavern ceiling and back into the endless void. I didn't even get to say thank you.

I see a faint light in front of me, my body propelling itself closer and closer towards it. The top of my head hits the light first. I feel a rush of cool air jet past me, like a splash of water on my face. My eyes snap open and I can see Whisperclaw looking over me. Pain courses through my back and stomach as I try to sit up. Out of the corner of my eye I notice Vanhiel standing up from among a pile of rubble. For the first time since he trans-formed, I can see anger appearing on his face.

"I warned you, God of Death." Vanhiel points his claw at Glimmer's dad. "Now, I will silence you for eternity."

I feel an eerie energy suddenly fill the room. At the same time, Vanhiel's finger becomes engulfed in blue light. Nobody can move. The light fires out of Vanhiel's finger in the shape of a small beam. It pierces straight through Glimmer's dad's chest. As the beam comes out of his back, I see Glimmer's dad literal-ly fall out of his fusion with the skeleton who called themselves Death. The skeleton whips around and catches Glimmer's dad in his arms as he falls. Even from this distance, I can see it in his eyes. Lifelessness. Glimmer's dad is dead.

"Shit." The skeleton says, small beams of white light crash-ing into it from the ceiling. "We still had 6 seconds left."

The beams of light physically pull the skeleton out of the room and up into the sky, where he disappears. I don't know what to say. I don't know what to do. I can't heal someone who's already dead. To make matters worse, Glimmer's dad was our only hope of leaving this alive.

"Dad!" All of us, Vanhiel included, look towards the cham-ber entrance.

Standing in the doorway is Glimmer, who drops to his knees with a look of complete disbelief on his face. All around him are knights clad in armor bearing the Sellsword Guild crest. I look down at the ground, lacking strength to stand. We failed him. We couldn't save his dad. We couldn't even save ourselves.

"Hahahaha!" Vanhiel's emotionless laughter fills my mind. "Yes! I did it! My ascension has been completed!"

"Ahhhhhhhhhh!" My eyes snap back to Glimmer who screams with all his might, tears streaming down his cheeks.

The room shakes violently. Glimmer grips his flute tightly. Plumes of thick, sparkling blue smoke fuming out of both ends, filling the entire chamber during Vanhiel's laughing. I can't see anything anymore except Whisperclaw, but I notice Glimmer hasn't stopped screaming.

"What's..." Whisperclaw helps me to my feet. "...what's happening?"

"I'm not sure." I answer her question as carefully as I can. "The way our luck has been these days, it can't be good."

It has to be something with Glimmer's magic, I'm sure of it. I can feel a massive amount of mana surging throughout the entire room, something that wasn't present until Glimmer showed up. Glimmer's screaming stops, and now I can hear Vanhiel again. He's not laughing anymore.

"What is this?" His quivering voice ricochets around my brain. "Who-no...what are you?"

A massive wind gust sweeps around the room. The smoke wraps around itself, like a tornado, centered directly in front of Glimmer. I feel my feet slip towards the spiraling smoke column. I can see that even Vanhiel is having trouble standing upright, digging his claws into the stone ground. Then the smoke collapses on itself, exploding outward. Me and Whisperclaw both get slammed to the ground and my vision becomes clouded again, for just a brief moment.

The smoke slowly reassembles in front of Glimmer, molding itself into a large human-like form. Glimmer's eyes are dull, almost soulless. He's not moving, but he's stopped screaming. The form solidifies into a young man with many human-like features: dark brown colored skin, bright pink hair with spiky ends, perfectly white teeth, standing around six feet tall. The smoke forms into elaborate, multi-colored clothing around the man. It forms into a small cape on his back. It gives him long white gloves that reach up to his elbow and slim black boots that reach to his knees. His eyes are two different colors, yellow and purple. He looks like a court jester.

"Hello reality!" The man yells out, striking a pose by sticking his hand on his hip and flaring his other hand into the air. "It's a pleasure to finally be alive!"

Chapter 48: Blue

(Jinx)

I don't feel right. Something is off. Something is missing. I can't hear anything. I can't feel anything. I think I hear voices, but they're muffled like underwater. I sense a rush of wind and something changes. The thing that was missing before is starting to come together. My body is taking form. The wind finally disperses and I stare at a horrible creature that I don't immediately recognize.

"Hello reality!" I yell, striking a pose to test my newly formed limbs. "It's a joy to finally be alive!"

Who are you? I hear a strangely familiar voice whisper softly behind me. I turn around and see a small snargle boy with sparkling blue skin. I feel like I've seen him before. I take a step towards him, my hand outstretching on its own. The boy's eyes are lifeless and filled with sorrow. It seems like his body no longer possesses a soul. The boy's hands reach up and touch mine. Suddenly, I feel myself lifted into the sky. The boy's body slams into mine and everything turns white.

(Glimmer)

"Glimmer!" Whisperclaw shouts.

I open my eyes and see that I'm floating in the sky. Multi-colored light floats off me in orbs and my skin is translucent. I can clearly remember what happened. After getting our supplies back, Dawn and the others led us to a secret door which led us to an underground chamber. There, we caught up with Loleo. I remember feeling a massive amount of mana the whole time we walked in. When we reached the room and rushed inside, I saw a beam of blue light cut directly through my dad's chest. For some reason though, I don't feel sad. If anything, I am more free than ever. I start laughing, laughing so hard that tears pour down my face.

"Did I miss the joke?" I see a creature covered in silver lunging at me in slow motion.

I notice that the creature's voice in my head sounds like Vanhiel and every urge to laugh leaves my body completely. Without thinking, I slam my hand into the creature's face. Multicolored sparks burst off as my hand contacts the creature and I hold it up. By his mana, I can tell it's Vanhiel. He looks smaller than before.

"Captain..." My eyes snap behind me and I can see Uriel drop his sword and fall to his hands and knees. "...Shane was right."

"Kid, are you still in there?" Loleo yells at me, as everyone slowly inches closer.

I see Renald lying motionless on the ground. Whisperclaw helps Ironvine limp over to his body. On the other side of the room, I see Goldenclaw and Liaz staring at me in pure amazement. Both look exhausted and Liaz seems like he's walked through the abyss. Behind them is a semi-transparent wall made of a black gaseous substance, separating us from a room filled with countless women and children. They are all chained to four obsidian pillars, which I can observe pulling raw mana directly from the women and children. It's being channeled into the ground. I can't tell what it's supposed to be doing. However, I can tell that if it keeps pulling mana at the same rate, those women and children will die soon.

I see Vanhiel twitch. The next thing I know, I'm slamming his head into the mana wall. I can't stop myself. I'm having fun. I see multicolored sparks flying off every time I make contact and laugh. I do it again and again, just to watch the sparks. One more time, is what I keep telling myself. I just want to see that blue again. The mana wall shatters, ending my fun and filling the room with screaming women and children.

"That didn't take much." I say, tossing Vanhiel into the pillar farthest from the innocent people in the room.

He crashes into the pillar, which splits and shatters into two pieces and crumbles on top of him. The mana surging around the room instantly dissipates when the pillar splits. I think about how convenient it would be if the chains didn't exist. In a puff of blue smoke, which fills the room for a moment, the chains disappear. They just aren't there anymore. I look back into the other room, at Loleo and the others who stare. They are obviously unsure of what to do.

"Get the women and children to safety." I say, my voice echoing across the room easily.

For a moment, nobody moves. Loleo shakes his head and yanks Uriel to his feet. He motions his hands and the other knights rush into the room, grabbing as many women and children as they can. As I go to check on Renald, I sense a powerful blast of mana flying towards me. I turn around and everything moves slowly again. I see a massive dragon made of blue electricity flying out of the rubble on top of Vanhiel and towards me. It's such a high concentration of mana that if it strikes, it will explode and kill all the defenseless people in the room.

I can imagine how funny it would be for the kids if the dragon turned into confetti and glowing streamers. It does. The electricity starts at the head and explodes into a mix of confetti and streamers that rain down on everyone. Through the falling party materials, I can see Vanhiel standing up now. His eyes are bloodshot and his body is a grotesque mixture of the yellow scaled draken he once was and the silver covered monster he had become. It's like the silver was peeled away, taking most of his scales with it but leaving behind the elongated claws and wings.

"Why?" He screams at me. "Why? Why? Why? Why didn't it work? I sacrificed everything! Everything!"

I think about standing over him and instantly am there, looking down on him. He looks back in shock and fear then drops to his knees, shivering. Tears of frustration pour down his face and onto the ground. I know that feeling well.

"That-that saber..." Vanhiel mumbles. "...That saber said I could win if I... sacrificed everything... so why?"

I want to feel sorry, I really do. However, seeing tears stream down Vanhiel's face fills me with unfiltered ecstasy. Before I even think about it, I've kicked Vanhiel into the wall at the back of the room. More sparks fly off my foot on contact and the kick shakes the entire room. I think about hitting him again and suddenly I'm punching him in the ribs. His body bounces off the wall with every hit and I can feel his scales breaking along with his bones. He screams more and more, louder and louder. I want him to suffer more, even more than he is now. This is so fun. Why have I never done this before?

I keep punching and punching. Each punch sends multi-colored sparks flying out of my fists. The crater in the wall gets deeper and deeper. Eventually, the different colored sparks disappear and are replaced by a thick crimson liquid that paints the room the same color. I can't think of anything else. I feel my joy fade and be replaced by anger. I don't want red. I want blue. The same blue that killed him. The same blue that took my father from me.

"Glimmer." I feel a heavy hand grab my shoulder, stopping me from punching the wall again. "He's already dead. There's nothing left."

I look behind me and am suddenly grabbed into a group hug by Ironvine and Whisperclaw. I see the light around me fade along with my ability to see the mana around me. My normal emotions also return, as if I had been possessed this whole time. Tears start to flow now. Tears mixed with confusion, regret, and disbelief. It's over. It's finally over, but he didn't make it. My dad didn't make it. After all these years of running, we finally understood each other, but it doesn't mean anything now. Hawk Wind, the King of bounty hunters, head of the House of Wind, and my father is dead. I feel light headed.

"Guys..." is the only word I can say before my legs give out and my vision fades.

Author's Note

Wow. I'm excited and burnt out at the same time. We did it. We completed our first official story arc. That's right, the Inner Circle Arc has come to a close. Honestly, I'm a little sad. This book ended up being way more sad than I thought it was going to be. Everyone died. I took a long time writing this one, mainly because I wanted it to be good, but also because I was nervous. I realize now that I had nothing to be nervous about. Sure, all the characters I spent months creating are dead now, but it all served a purpose. Most of that purpose won't pay off until much later, but at least I was able to set the tone for the rest of the series. Expect a lot more death, a lot more heartbreak, a lot more... everything. Like always, I'm just rambling on. I'm sure you guys want me to talk about the story a little bit. The first thing I should talk about is probably Renald. He and Glimmer had the most development of everyone in this book. A lot of their development early on had to do with each other too, which I find interesting. I'm excited to explore their dynamic in the next arc, especially since everyone else knows Renald might be a vampire now. Speaking of, Renald slowly became more and more vampiric over the course of the book. Up until he drinks Ash's blood, which causes one of the most influential scenes in the whole book. In my opinion, of course. I feel like Renald and Glimmer mirror each other a lot in this book, although in different ways. Renald slowly gives into his rage and allows his vampire side to start consuming him in order to gain the power to help everyone. Glimmer is the most irritated we've ever seen him. Because he doesn't have his flute, Glimmer doesn't think he has the power to help. Iron-vine was the most helpful in this book, by a long shot. His relationship with Celestria is getting interesting as well, if I may say so myself. Other than that, I don't feel that there's too much that I should touch on for right now. Book 4 should be released around Thanksgiving of this year. We will be starting a new arc, so you can look forward to that. In the meantime, follow me on Twitter at Valerius Laborum to catch the latest updates when I post them.

With much love from your prince,
Valrius Laborum

Also by Valerius Laborem

The Black Raven Saga
The Tower of Abell
The House of Wind
The Inner Circle

About the Author

Hey there! I'm Valerius Laborem, a 21-year-old daydreamer soaking up the vibes in the good ol' United States. Life in my world is like a constant party, with nine siblings (three bros and six awesome sisters) adding all sorts of chaos and color to the mix. I'm all about that music life – whether I'm jamming out to tunes or crafting my own. My big dream? Becoming a song-writer and weaving tales through melodies. But here's the real deal: my heart beats for worldbuilding. It all started back in the day, playing tabletop RPGs and getting lost in epic fantasy nov-els like "The Lion, The Witch, and The Wardrobe." I'm a Pisces, born on February 20th, 2003, swimming through life's waves and finding inspiration in every ebb and flow. My true passion lies in creating worlds, breathing life into characters, and letting my imagination run wild on the pages. Come join me on this journey – where every word is a star and every note is a heart-beat.

Milton Keynes UK
Ingram Content Group UK Ltd.
UKHW031256251024
450245UK00001B/26